I took both her hands in my right hand and patted them gently with my left. "Don't worry, Chantal, I'll find your brother."

I knew I would. David wasn't trying to create a new identity for himself. At least I didn't think so. Those are the kind that are hard to find. This looked like a Julius Blumberg case. But for Chantal Montez I was prepared to take on a Julius Blumberg case. I was prepared to do a lot more than that.

As it turned out I was wrong. It wasn't a Julius Blumberg case. Oh, I found David Turley all right. Fast Dead Murdered. But it wasn't a Julius Blumberg case. It was a tantalizing puzzle.

I didn't solve the puzzle until I learned the answer to one key question.

The answer came from a dead man.

ANSWER FROM A DEAD MAN

GEORGE CRONIN

CONDOR

NEW YORK

ANSWER FROM A DEAD MAN

CONDOR

CONDOR edition published February 1978

All Rights Reserved
Copyright © 1978 by George Cronin

ISBN 0-89516-021-8
Library of Congress Catalog Number: 77-90457

Printed in the United States of America

CONDOR PUBLISHING COMPANY, INC.
521 Fifth Avenue
New York, N.Y. 10017

To Marvin Kaye with many thanks

Chapter 1

I received $100,000 for the Parrish case. The money enabled me to resolve never again to accept one of those Julius Blumberg cases I hated. It also provided me with an opportunity to take my first vacation in a couple of years.

I went to Tortuga. I planned to stay for perhaps a month of fishing and diving. Instead of relaxation I found there a nightmare of intrigue and murder. Against my will, I became embroiled in a bloody scenario that began with my discovery of a mutilated body on Twelve Mile Beach. It ended with the exposure of a lottery fraud scheme of gigantic proportions, and the disgrace of a prominent international financier. After I cleaned up the mess, and pocketed another $100,000, I fled from the island three weeks early, returning to the clammy heat but relative peace and quiet of Manhattan.

I could hear the phone in my apartment ringing before the doors of the elevator opened. I hate telephones and the demands they make, but I am as much a slave to them as anyone else. I opened the door, hurried into the living room, and picked up the receiver.

"Hello?"

"Virgil," said Chantal Montez in that velvet voice I recognized immediately, "I need your help. Can you get over here right away?"

She wasn't the kind of woman you could say no to. At least I couldn't. "I'm leaving now," I said.

She had been Parrish's mistress. My investigation of his death had required me to interview her. I did. Once. But her beauty, her courage, her quiet endurance had made an indelible impression on me.

She opened the door to her suite at the Phoenix herself. She wasn't as I had remembered her. Not exactly. She looked better. The effects of the blow she had taken when she heard of Parrish's death had worn off slightly. Her huge black eyes were luminous and clear. She had a double set of eyelashes. When she makes movies those eyelashes must present quite a technical problem to the cameraman. He probably has to resort to heavy use of pinpoint lights to do them justice.

"Virgil," she said, "I'm so glad you're here. I never thanked you for finding Bob's killer." She was dressed simply in French jeans and a black man-tailored shirt that matched her raven hair and contrasted nicely with her pale translucent skin. She wasn't completely herself. Ugly worry lines etched faint trails in her high forehead. "*Gracias*, Virgil," she said.

She sat next to me on a high-backed sofa in a sunny, pleasant room decorated in neutral tones. Her body exuded a light, sweet scent that seemed to come from the skin itself. "You don't have to thank me, Chantal."

"I'm glad I have," she said. "I called your office but your answering service said you were on vacation for

8

a month. I called you at home several times, but no one answered. Today I called because I was desperate. I'm so glad I managed to get you."

"Tell me about it."

"It's my brother, Virgil. He's missing." There was a catch in her voice and her eyes were moist. I handed her my handkerchief.

She blew her nose. "I'm sorry, Virgil. It's just that I'm so worried. Go ahead and ask me your questions." She had balled up the handkerchief in her right fist and was squeezing it. "I called the police and was told they wouldn't handle it."

Missing Persons won't get involved if the person missing is over eighteen and there are no indications of foul play. "How long has he been missing?"

"Three days now. It was three days this noon. I said good-bye to him right in this room on Friday."

"Where was he going?"

"I'm not sure exactly. He was going to do some shopping—we were supposed to fly to the coast that night. My play closed last Sunday. I had some things to clear up in New York, but I was due back in L.A. yesterday. Tomorrow is the first day of David's vacation. He was going to spend a week of it with me out there."

"David? His name's David? David Montez?"

She smiled. "No, not Montez. Turley. That's my real name, Eileen Turley. I became Chantal Montez thirty years ago when I came over here to the Big Apple from Cedarwood, New Jersey, and started singing with Ephraim Camacho."

"Camacho? Yes I vaguely remember that. You started with him."

"I was only fifteen."

Her looks were so exotic that I never associated her

9

with a stage name. Chantal Montez seemed to suit her perfectly. "How come . . ." I began.

"More people don't know about my mundane provenance?" she interrupted. "The buffs do. It's not a secret, but we don't broadcast it. How come most people don't know that Gary Clark's real name is Schlomo Biderman, and that he comes from the Bronx?"

"Gary Clark, the cowboy star?"

"Yes, we're co-starring in a movie that starts a week from tomorrow."

"He comes from the Bronx?" It was news to me. He looked like the original tall Texan. "His real name is . . ."

"Yes, Schlomo Biderman."

"But your Spanish . . . ?"

"I don't speak Spanish, Virgil. I just have a few words and phrases that I've used so often that they're second nature to me now."

Things are never what they seem to be. People are rarely who you think they are. "You say your brother's on vacation," I said, bringing us back to more pertinent matters. "Where does he work?"

"He's an accountant at Post-McBride."

I looked at her quizzically. You didn't expect the exotic Chantal Montez to have a brother who worked for one of the country's largest public accounting firms. Of course, it made a difference when you knew his real name was David Turley. It almost made sense.

"David's not at all like me," she said in explanation. "He's almost an old fuddy-duddy. He was a straight-A student in college. He's neat and precise you can set your clock by him. He's so only twenty-five and he's a C.P.A. already."

"Does he live here with you?"

10

"No, he has his own apartment. I have a key for it."

"Have you gone up there?"

"No. I've called him and left messages—he has one of those automatic telephone answering devices—but I haven't heard from him."

"Young men of his age have been known to disappear for a few days. Maybe he just took off for the weekend. Maybe he'll be back tomorrow." It was Monday, July 5, a holiday.

"No," she said firmly. "David is quite responsible. I told you we were going to the coast Friday night. He'd never disappoint me by cancelling out. If he did cancel out it would have to be for something extraordinarily important, and he'd tell me about it. He'd give me a full explanation."

"Does he live alone?"

"Yes."

"Does he have a girl friend?"

"No. He's very active with women and quite popular with them, but he hasn't focused his attentions on just one in quite a while."

"Do you have a picture of him? A small one I could carry with me?"

It was a studio portrait, wallet size. He was as beautiful as she was. He had her large intelligent black eyes. His heart-shaped facial lines tapered from Indian cheekbones to frame sensuous lips. The jawline was clean-cut and ran right up to his ear lobes. His skin was pearly and translucent like hers. His black hair was thick and shaggy, and was cut relatively short. I put the picture in my pocket. "How tall is he?" I asked.

"A little shorter than you," she replied. "Six-foot-two, and he weighs two-hundred-ten pounds."

"Any scars, tattoos, distinguishing marks?"

"No. Yes. He has a small scar on the inside of his

11

right hand pinky. Oh, Virgil, this is awful. I raised that boy from the time he was eight years old. He's all I have in the world." She was dabbing at her eyes with my handkerchief again.

"Your folks are gone?"

"Yes. He's my only living relative. It wasn't easy raising him—children can be smothered by famous relatives. I did everything I could to avoid that. David went his own way. He's his own man. That's why he avoided glamour and became an accountant. Only now I was hoping he'd go into business with me. We had pretty well decided to form our own production company. I would handle the artistic side and he would look after the business details. And now he's God knows where!" she wailed. She had begun to pick savagely at my handkerchief with her teeth.

I took both her hands in my right hand and patted them gently with my left. "Don't worry, Chantal, I'll find your brother."

I knew I would. David wasn't trying to create a new identity for himself. At least I didn't think so. Those are the kind that are hard to find. This looked like a Julius Blumberg case. But for Chantal Montez I was prepared to take on a Julius Blumberg case. I was prepared to do a lot more than that.

As it turned out I was wrong. It wasn't a Julius Blumberg case. Oh, I found David Turley all right. Fast. Dead. Murdered. But it wasn't a Julius Blumberg case. It was a tantalizing puzzle.

I didn't solve the puzzle until I learned the answer to one key question.

The answer came from a dead man.

Chapter 2

THE cabbie was surly. He gave me the evil eye. "Where to?" he asked. I gave him David Turley's address in the eighties.

"How do you want to get there?"

This was a new game in town. It had started about a decade earlier and was now endemic. They'd ask you how you wanted to get some place. You'd tell them. Then (if they knew how to get there themselves) they'd give you a half-dozen reasons why your route was a poor choice, offering at least two or three alternates that any sensible person would prefer. I avoided all this by using my standard response: "Whatever way you think is fastest."

He glared at me, threw down his flag savagely, and rabbited off with enough force to pin me to the back seat for a block. He was getting even with me for not playing the game.

The character of the neighborhoods changed as we went uptown. The dogs told the story. The East sixties were inhabited by mincing, styled puffballs at the ends of leashes held by disinterested maids. Further up, in Turley's neighborhood, noble-looking hounds held sway, leashed to strollers with balloons strung to the handles.

The building was one of those nondescript piles of white brick erected in the thirties. There was no doorman on duty. The apartment itself was comfortable in terms of available space, three large rooms not including kitchen and bath, but its furnishings left something to be desired. An interior designer might have waxed enthusiastic over the different patterned metals and the play of geometric forms and lines in gray, silver, and natural wood tones. I found it too spare and cold.

I toured the apartment quickly to get a feel for it and then I spent a couple of hours giving it a thorough toss. I overlooked nothing. I emptied and sifted the contents of all the cans in the kitchen. I checked the seams of all the upholstery and felt around the inside of any of it that looked as if it might have been tampered with. I found nothing of interest but a strange list that, enclosed in a manila folder, had been taped to the underside of the bottom drawer of a dresser in the bedroom.

The list had been typed on an executive typewriter and said:

```
          RE: J.H. and R.J.
          Atlas Laundry
          M&M Butchers
          Freedom Maintenance
```

I had no idea what the list meant, but I knew it was important—important enough for David Turley to try to hide it. Was it important enough to explain his disappearance?

I didn't know. I copied the information from the

list into my pocket notebook, and returned the folder and its contents to the underside of the drawer.

On the way home I stopped off at a deli on Broadway and bought some pumpernickel and Westphalian ham. At home, I made a couple of sandwiches and ate them, washed down with two bottles of Ringnes.

I called Chantel, told her what I had, and what I was going to do with it.

I turned in before twelve.

I still hadn't recovered from my trip to Tortuga.

Chapter 3

WALKER ("Wally") Post was at ease amid the rose-wood furnishings and calm pastels of Post-McBride's executive suite. His three-piece fawn colored tweed suit, his regular features under his silver gray hair, and his meerschaum all attested to the calm security he felt in his role as president of one of the country's most distinguished public accounting firms. Not for him the firm's unspoken dress code—dark blue single-breasted suit, white shirt, plain dark tie, black shoes and socks. Post chose to dress and act more like an English country gentleman than the man ultimately responsible for the accuracy of the books and records of some of the most prestigious corporations in America.

I had met him a few years before when I was tracking down an executive officer of the First National Trust who had absconded with over $250,000 that belonged to the bank's depositors. I eventually found the thief, broke, working in a concession at a dog track in Florida. I was surprised that Post remembered me, and gratified that he had me ushered into his presence immediately.

"This is most distressing news, Mr. Fletcher. David's a brilliant young man, conscientious, imaginative, and a horse for work. We made him a senior accountant after just six months, and although he's only been here three years now, we've just about decided to make him a manager. How can we help?"

"I'd like to have a list of the accounts he works on, including the names of the principals of the organizations, and the name of the person in the organization that he deals with most frequently."

"I don't know if we can give you exactly what you want in exactly the way you want it. When we hire a junior accountant we give him as much diversified experience as possible. When he becomes a senior we try to give him different accounts to broaden him even more. It wouldn't be unusual for David never to have dealt with the same firm twice. That wouldn't be true if he worked for our management advisory service, but he didn't. He was in our auditing division."

"But you can give me a list of all the firms he has audited since he's been working here?"

"That should be easy to do. I'll get Bill Avildsen in here. He's Dave's manager. He should be able to give you what you want."

Avildsen looked like an accountant, a gray, dusty little man with hard little eyes framed by rimless spectacles. He moused deferentially before Post.

He had a neatly prepared folder for David Turley that included schedules of audits due, estimated completion dates, and actual completion dates. I glanced briefly at the schedules and noted that Turley usually had his assignments completed well before the deadline date. The master list of his accounts was neatly typed and included the name of the organization, its address and telephone number. Next to the name of each account, there was neatly printed at least one set

17

of initials, and in most cases two or more sets. "What are these initials?" I asked Avildsen.

"Those are the initials of the junior accountants assigned to the audits," he said. "Just about all of our work is done on a rotating basis. I make up these schedules about three months in advance and tentatively assign them to the seniors. As juniors are freed up I assign them to the audits. When I do assign them I keep track of them by putting their initials next to the name of the firm they've been assigned to audit. I also keep a master list of assignments on a wall chart," he went on proudly. "If you'd like to see it it's in my . . ."

"I don't think that will be necessary," I said. I'd met his type before. His office would look like a War Room, with graphs and multicolored charts on the wall, and time studies in the filing cabinet. It was up or out at Post-McBride and Avildsen was covering all the bases. Going back to June 1975, Turley had been assigned about thirty audits. "It seems like he's been given a lot of work to do."

"It is Post-McBride's way of giving our staff diversified experience," said Avildsen. "You see, we here at Post-McBride . . ."

"Mr. Post has already explained the diversification stuff to me. It still seems like a lot."

"Yes. Well in Dave's case he was started out on mostly large accounts, accounts that require several months to audit. He was assigned to me last year to get experience with our small customers. You're right about one thing. He puts out a lot of work. High quality work," Avildsen added, glancing toward Post for approval.

Post nodded and smiled encouragingly. Apparently David Turley was a fair-haired boy at Post-McBride.

Starting from June 1975, I went over the list more

slowly. The names on the list appeared to be of small manufacturers of paper boxes or valves, or the like. Most of them were located in the wilds of the Bronx, or Queens. The next-to-last name on the list rang a bell—Janus House. The initials "G.L." were next to it, but had been scratched out. The due date for completion of the audit was June 30. It had been completed on June 28. "Why were these initials scratched out?" I asked.

Avildsen looked puzzled for a moment, then brightened. "Garth Lambert, one of our juniors was supposed to do the work on it, but we had to let him go. We have a high attrition rate here. He'd done most of the work on Janus House before he left. Dave went in and handled the closing conference himself."

"What is a closing conference?"

"We go over our audit findings with the concerned people in the organization."

"Is it unusual for a senior to handle a closing conference?"

"Not at all. Usually he's accompanied by the juniors who did the on-site work."

"In this case there was only one junior."

"Yes," said Avildsen.

"What kind of an outfit is Janus House?" I asked.

"I can answer that better than Bill," said Post. "Janus House is one of our charity accounts."

"Charity accounts?"

"Yes, we audit some nonprofit organizations free of charge, as a community service. Janus House is a drug free rehabilitation program. My wife knows the director of Janus House, Marianne Sprague, and has helped her raise funds. In fact I'm on the board of directors. The audits don't cost us that much in terms of time, and when you consider the tax write-off . . ."

"They cost nothing?" I asked.

19

"Well, the cost is modest," said Post.

I had to hand it to David Turley. He knew how to climb. It wouldn't hurt for Post to know that he had *personally* expedited the audit of a charity account brought to the firm by Post himself. No doubt Turley had found some subtle way to call Post's attention to his zeal. "What exactly is involved in an audit of a place like Janus House?"

"It's fairly routine," said Avildsen, "but it can be time-consuming. We have to certify any financial statements they submit to government agencies to get funds. We certify it for the board of directors also, of course."

"Yes, indeed," said Post.

"Were there any unusual findings for Janus House?"

"I haven't see——" Avildsen started.

"I have. There weren't," interrupted Post. "It's one of the accounts in which I take a personal interest, Mr. Fletcher."

"Do you mind if I take a look at the work papers and the latest audit report for Janus House?"

"I don't mind, Mr. Fletcher, but I would like to know why. We'll cooperate with you all the way in your attempt to find David, but of what use is it to you?"

"It's just a starting place," I lied. "It is the last piece of work Dave Turley completed." I didn't know if the initials J.H. that were on the list I found taped to the underside of the bottom drawer in Turley's dressing room stood for Janus House. Even if I knew they did, I wouldn't tell Post. Not unless I had to. I didn't have to.

"Normally I wouldn't do this, Mr. Fletcher, but I remember your work on the First National Trust case, and your reputation is good. If David's disappearance is linked in any way to his work at Janus House I hope you'll let me know. I am personally interested. If you like I'll call Marianne and tell her she can expect to hear from you."

"I'll do whatever I can to keep you informed. I'd appreciate your calling Miss Sprague for me," I said.

"Bill, find some work space for Mr. Fletcher and give him the Janus House files. If you need any help after this, call Bill directly. If there are any problems Bill can't handle, don't hesitate to contact me. I don't anticipate any such problems, do you, Bill?"

"No sir, Mr. Post, of course not." He looked worried. He wasn't used to being this close to the boss.

Chapter 4

MOST laymen think that accounting is an exact science. The myth is probably based on what the layman knows about balancing books. When books are said to be balanced, it seems that some exact scientific measurements have been taken to determine that fact. What the layman doesn't know is that the device that allows books to be balanced, double-entry bookkeeping, also makes things seem "balanced" when the fact is that the same error has been entered on both sides of a ledger.

I didn't have to know anything about accounting to look for what I wanted in Post-McBride's Janus House file. The spare cubicle that Avildsen gave me for work space contained nothing but a desk, a chair, and an empty filing cabinet. On top of the desk was a telephone and a calculator. The desk was empty save for a mammoth bottle of aspirin in the lower left-hand drawer. According to the label, the bottle contained 10,000 tablets when it was bought. I opened the bottle and peered into it. It looked empty. I put the cap back on and shook the bottle. Something rattled faintly. I removed the cap again, and emptied the contents of the bottle into my hand. A trickle of dusty white powder and one lone aspirin fell into my palm.

I returned the aspirin to the bottle and the bottle to the drawer. As I wiped the aspirin powder from my hands Avildsen came into the cubicle with the Janus House file.

"Whose office is this?" I asked.

"Was, Mr. Fletcher."

"O.K., was," I conceded.

"Garth Lambert used it," he said.

"The guy who was fired before he could do the Janus House closing conference? Why exactly was he fired?"

"He just didn't measure up to our standards, Mr. Fletcher. He'd been here three years. He wasn't good enough to be promoted to senior accountant. It's up or out here. He will be replaced by a new junior accountant who we hope will become a senior accountant, a manager, and so on up through Post-McBride."

He sounded like the voice-over on a recruiting film.

"Who actually fired Lambert?"

"David Turley made the recommendation."

"Were there any hard feelings?"

"About the firing? No, none at all. When we hire people here we make them aware of our attrition rate. This is a very prestigious place for an accountant to work. Even those we fire are in demand. In Garth's case, I think he was grateful to be let go."

"Grateful?"

"Yes, he was a low-key person and he didn't really like the long hours and pressure around here."

I didn't know Garth Lambert but it was obvious that something had gotten to him. You don't become an aspirin freak for no reason at all. It probably was

23

the job. All of the aspirin freaks I knew held high-pressure jobs.

Avildsen left and I pored over the Janus House file. The stationery told me that Marianne Sprague was only the codirector of Janus House. She shared the honor with one Robie Jeanette. The file contained an alphabetical listing of the vendors doing business with Janus House.

I found Atlas Laundry. It was located in the Bronx. Freedom Maintenance and M&M Butchers were also listed. Their addresses were both uptown, in Harlem. The list that I had found in Turley's apartment was no longer a complete mystery. "J.H." was Janus House. "R.J." was Robie Jeanette. Atlas Laundry, Freedom Maintenance, and M&M Butchers were Janus House vendors. Of course, I still didn't know the significance of the list, why it had been drawn up in the first place, and why it was hidden in the bedroom of my client's missing brother.

None of the organizations on the list appeared to be corporations. I called my contacts in the County Clerk's offices of both Manhattan and the Bronx, and had them track down any partnership papers on file for the three firms. I was lucky. They were all partnerships.

The agreements had all been drawn up within two months of each other in the spring of 1968: April 4 for the butcher, April 19 for the laundry, and May 17 for the maintenance outfit.

M&M had three partners: Nicole Percy, Luke Stackhouse, and Brian Percy. The laundry had two partners: Clyde Lincoln and Pearl Jackson. The maintenance outfit had three partners: Pearl Jackson, Nicole Percy, and Earl Washington.

The total amount paid to M&M in calendar year

24

1975 was $63,101.50; to Atlas Laundry, $49,849.74; to Freedom Maintenance, $37,515.85.

Avildsen looked startled when I returned the file.

"Through already?" he asked. "It's been less than . . ."

"Ten minutes," I said.

I left. I didn't have time for small talk.

The case was getting interesting.

Chapter 5

THE cab went west on 34th Street to Eighth Avenue
and then turned north. It picked its way like a broken
field runner through the traffic on the Minnesota
Strip, the sleazy area from 42nd to 52nd Streets that
is the city's largest vice supermarket. It was hot and
humid. The Strip seemed more drab and gray than
usual despite the throngs that swarmed on its side-
walks. Slack-jawed out-of-towners hoping for cheap
thrills looked fearfully at the hard-eyed hookers and
their flashily-dressed procurers. Fast-talking three-
card monte hustlers vied with glib con men and rip-
off artists to relieve the Strip's visitors of the contents
of their wallets. Dingy pornography shops stood
cheek by jowl with cheap massage parlors and fetid
topless bars. The chicken hawks were out in force,
lounging furtively near the penny arcades.

We traveled up Broadway past the welfare hotels
whose fragile residents were taking the air in their
walkers and turned left onto a street in the upper sev-
enties. I got out in front of the Janus House—three
brick buildings in a block of nineteenth-century flats
with elaborate cornices and arched and bay windows.

A sign over the entrance of the building in bold black letters on a white background said: "Janus House." Written underneath this in black script was: "Always aware of our past, we can face our future."

I breathed a sigh of relief as I stepped into the air-conditioned entrance foyer. It was no day to be on the streets. A young black woman with a round plump face was operating the switchboard, which stood against the far wall of the alcove at the back of the entrance foyer. Her eyes were older than sin, and as empty as the backs of tombstones.

I told her who I was and that I wanted to see Marianne Sprague. She told me I was expected and directed me to Sprague's office. It was on the top floor of the building in a secluded wing of the house whose hallway held a duplicator, a stamp machine, filing cabinets, and two desks placed near the doors of what looked like adjoining rooms. There was another door at the end of the hallway that probably led to stairs going to the rear entrance of the house.

There was no one at the first desk. Behind the second sat a plump, pink-cheeked woman. The plaque on her desk read: "Mrs. Dowd." "Hello, Mr. Fletcher," she said. "Go right in. Miss Sprague is expecting you. She was pointing to the room closest to her desk.

The walls of Marianne Sprague's office were painted bright psychedelic orange. I hate orange. Every piece of plastic gimcrackery made in twentieth-century America is produced in orange. You might not be able to get it in blue, or yellow, or green, or red, or any other color, but you could always get it in orange. Three of the walls were decorated with photographs of Sprague posed with celebrities—pols, entertainers, writers, and journalists. The fourth held her framed professional diplomas. She was a lawyer, an M.D., and a psychiatrist—three strikes against her as far as I was concerned.

The rug was a deep nubby wool in vibrant yellow. The windows were covered by drapes that matched the rug and a long white leather couch was placed near the windows. In front of the couch was a low wooden table as long as the couch. On the other side of the table stood comfortable armchairs covered with a nubby floral print material.

Sprague's costume matched the garishly decorated office. She was swaddled in a long, embroidered, slavic peasant dress, and she was weighted with chic thrift-shop jewelry—huge doughnutty gold earrings, chunky stone rings on two fingers of each hand, heavy bangles on each wrist, and a chunky old necklace down the open neck of her dress. With each movement she made she clinked, chimed, or rattled. Sometimes, she did all three.

"Well, Mr. Fletcher, I heard from Mr. Post that you might be in touch with me. Something about a missing person?"

There were lines in her forehead and the flesh under her chin had begun to sag. Her face, which looked scorched by hard work, was flushed and lightly freckled. Her face was narrow, her features thin. But she was not unattractive: the body under her peasant dress hinted at voluptuousness, her smoke-gray eyes held a certain passionate intensity, and her flyaway art nouveau hair was a spectacular flaming red.

I nodded.

Before I could say anything she went on: "An accountant who worked on our books or something, wasn't it?"

I nodded again.

"A Mr. Tully, I believe?" Her voice was clear and

resonant. Her words were impatient to come out, although she seemed to examine them and adjust their nuances before letting them go. Then they all burst out at once, floundering and bumping into each other.

"Turley," I said.

"Oh. Turley. I'm afraid I won't be able to help you at all. I'm responsible for the treatment aspects of the Janus House program. My codirector, Mr. Jeanette, handles the business end of things." When she said "Mr. Jeanette" she spit it out as if she couldn't stand the name on her tongue or its sound in her ears. "What do you know about drug addiction, Mr. Fletcher?"

"Only what I read in the papers."

"What do you know about Janus House?"

I knew more about her than I did about Janus House, and all I knew about her was impressions I had received from newspaper articles about her that I had skimmed in the past. As I recalled, she had a talent for self-promotion and the flashy gesture. Once I had seen her on a late night TV panel show. I'd watched it for perhaps ten or fifteen minutes, and had been impressed by her verbal aggressiveness and style. "Very little," I said.

"Heroin addiction is the single most important problem facing this country today!"

She said it flatly and dogmatically. I wasn't going to argue with her. She was as zealous as a blackrobe preaching to the heathen.

"Janus House is a laboratory, Mr. Fletcher. A laboratory where we've conducted experiments and have come up with what we think is the answer to the problem of heroin addiction. It's not an easy answer, but it's not an easy problem. All of our residents are volunteers, Mr. Fletcher, but not volunteers in the usual sense. They chose Janus House as the best of quite a few uninviting alternatives all of which demand that they surrender their main reason for living, their drug habit. Giving it up isn't easy. It means pain and deprivation. Of course to maintain the habit would invariably mean prison, or death, or both."

She paused to take a breath. I didn't know what to make of her pitch. I did know I didn't want to hear her out to the end. "As long as Mr. Jeanette handles business matters, perhaps . . ."

"Forgive me, Mr. Fletcher," she said firmly. "I'm afraid you'll have to be patient and listen to my spiel. Anyone who steps into my office is a captive audience." She ran the fingers of both hands through her red hair, and closed her gray eyes for a moment. "I'll take you to Mr. Jeanette in a little bit. Now, let's see, where was I?" She bit her lower lip with white, needle-sharp little teeth.

"Your patients are volunteers but not really volunteers."

"Oh, yes." Her eyes snapped open again. "Heroin addiction has reached epidemic proportions, Mr. Fletcher. Hundreds of thousands, perhaps millions, of our young people are hooked on this insidious habit. Society must be protected from these addicts, and they must be protected from themselves. By the way, I wish you wouldn't call members of the Janus House community 'patients.' I slip sometimes myself and call them residents."

"What term do you prefer?" I asked.

"Oh," she said vaguely, "any acceptable alternative will suffice. We try to use the word 'members.'"

"O.K.," I said. "Members."

She smiled and her thin mouth seemed a random slash across her face. It emphasized her narrow features and made them seem even more linear. "Bear with me, Mr. Fletcher," she said. "I'm afraid you're dealing with a zealot."

"I've already come to that conclusion," I replied.

"Most psychiatrists think of addicts as beyond hope. Psychoanalysis doesn't work for them. As I already pointed out, they're not really volunteers and so they're often nakedly hostile to treatment. Occasionally an addict might seem prepared to accept traditional psychoanalysis, but usually they are overcome by despair and drop out of treatment."

"And your program has no dropouts?" I asked. As long as I was her captive audience, I felt better engaging in a dialogue than sitting as silent as a stone, listening to a monologue.

"Remarkably few when compared to other programs," she said. "Of course, our members screen the addicts who apply for admission to the program."

"How do they screen them?"

"Primarily we look for some kind of emotion—rage or despair, or some sign that they're in touch with their feelings. We don't want people looking for three hots and a cot."

"You don't take what they have to say at face value?"

"No, you can't do that with an addict. They're very manipulative. They'll lie, cheat, provoke, attack, do anything to gain control. At Janus House we remain in control."

"We?"

"Myself and my staff. But, of course, most of my staff are members who worked their way up through the Janus House organization."

"They're therapists?"

"Not all of my therapists are ex-addicts, but some of them are. It's the highest goal one of our members can attain—at least within Janus House."

"Isn't it unusual to have untrained people provide therapy?"

"They're not untrained. I have trained them."

"I see."

"You're not impressed, are you? You have to understand that addicts are lonely, alienated people with fragmented personalities. In order to be cured they have to learn to trust."

"Trust you?"

"Not me personally, Mr. Fletcher, but Janus House, the idea of Janus House. It's easier for them to trust ex-addicts of course."

"What is the idea of Janus House?"

"You know our motto?"

"Always aware of our past, we can face our future," I declaimed.

"That's it," she said. "If the addict is *aware, really aware* of his past, then he can *face, really face* his future."

When people begin to underline their spoken words I begin to get suspicious. "Tell me something, Miss Sprague, how many members have been processed through your program?"

"That's hard to say. This is only our mother house. We have six other houses in New York City. We're opening two more. Someday, we hope to operate on a nationwide basis. I'd say since 1967, when we started, we've dealt with at least five thousand addicts."

"How many have been cured?"

"That's hard to say. It depends how long they were in the program and how you define 'cure.'"

I seemed to have hit on the right approach for cutting the interview short. "The five thousand addicts that you mentioned, did they all go through the program?"

"That number . . . I'm not too sure of the number

32

. . . but, yes that number referred to those who completed the program."

"How many have started the program?"

"I'm really not sure, exactly . . . you see when we started we had no funds . . . couldn't keep records . . . and of course we've made changes . . ."

"Was it ten thousand?"

"I don't know."

"Fifteen thousand? Eight thousand?"

"I'm . . . I'm not really sure."

"How do you define 'cure'?" I asked.

"There's no simplistic answer to that, my friend." Her confusion was gone and replaced by cold self-assurance. "At any rate the complexities involved in arriving at such a definition are beyond the comprehension of a layman." Doctors and lawyers always say that when you put them in a corner. "I'm afraid I've wasted too much of your time, Mr. Fletcher. Let's go see my codirector."

She said "codirector" in a strange cold voice.

It seemed as though she couldn't even bear to speak Robie Jeanette's name.

Chapter 6

JEANETTE'S office was next to hers. She rapped on its
door twice and walked right in. The room's atmosphere became as frosty as the inside of an unheated
igloo.

"Mr. Jeanette," she said curtly, "this is Mr. Fletcher.
He's a private detective. He's looking for a missing
person." She glared at Jeanette malevolently. His look
was no friendlier. "An accountant who worked on our
books. I hope you can help him." She turned on her
heel and slammed the door behind her.

Jeanette was sitting on a stool at a small bar covered with red leather that was in the far corner of the
room. He was sprawled comfortably with his back
against it, leaning on his elbows. Standing in front of
him between his legs, her arms twined around his
neck, was a striking coffee-colored woman at least six
feet tall. She was sloe-eyed and dressed in a red and
white floral print dress that looked as though it had
been vulcanized onto her body. "Come ri' over cheer
wi' me, Fletcher," he said. "This heah's my secretary,
Miss Billy Jefferson. Say hello to Mr. Fletcher,
honey."

"Hello, Mr. Fletcher," she said in a voice like molten gold.

"Yo'll take care of business now, Billy," he said.

We both followed her with our eyes as she stalked from the room as gracefully as a panther. Her figure would make a monk turn his head.

"Well, alrighty, Fletcher," said Jeanette with a deep throaty chuckle. "When ah was growin' up yard-dog poor in South Carolina, ah never did think ah'd wind up with all this. Yehyehyehyeh, man." He pointed toward the door through which Billy had just left and then made a sweeping gesture that encompassed the whole room.

The decor of the room was tastelessly expensive. The dark walls were aglow with the reflections of rose-gold mosaic mirrors and glassy beading. The floor was covered with a white rug with a nap as thick as the greens at Burning Tree. The windows stood behind floor-to-ceiling silver aluminum blinds, and one wall held a recessed system with a TV, a stereo, cabinets, and shelves. The shelves were covered by fierce-looking African sculptures. Underneath the wall an oversized orange ottoman and paired lounge chairs were flanked by suede cubes and rectangles. In the corner opposite the bar several rattan peacock armchairs were placed casually around an elaborate ziggurat-motif commode and coffee table. There was no desk in the room. I could appreciate Jeanette's wondering tone. The room was a long way from South Carolina. "It's amazing what you can pick up at flea markets these days," I said.

Jeanette's head sat like a cannonball directly on top of his shoulders. He had no neck. His eyes rolled up to the ceiling. The whites were as bright and shiny as a fresh coat of high-gloss enamel. He boomed out a ho-ho laugh as loud as the one used to lure customers into the fun houses at amusement parks. "You O.K., Fletcher, you know that," he wheezed. "How about a splash, man?" He dug me in the ribs with his elbow, winked, and pounded me on the back with a hand as big as a squash racket.

"Wild Turkey on the rocks," I said.

He reached over the bar and selected a bottle of Wild Turkey from the impressive collection of liquors that were shelved there. He poured a generous slug into an old-fashioned glass and gave it to me. "Next best thing to white whiskey," he said. "Is it David Turley you're looking for, Mr. Fletcher?"

He asked the question in a well-modulated voice, deep and with no trace of the raspiness and southern-fried accent he had used before. His manner was still open and friendly but was now full of a worldly grace.

"Yes. When did you see him last?"

"I saw him last Monday. We had our closing conference."

"Any problems?"

"With what, Mr. Fletcher?"

"With the audit."

"None that he told me about."

"He didn't mention any of Janus House's vendors? Didn't mention anything about problems with them?"

"She-e-e-e-e-t, man. Ah'm aimin' ta get knee-walkin' drunk today an yo'll gotta come roun' heah askin' foolish questions!"

He had reverted to his cornpone accent. Was I getting to him? "Did you ever hear of Atlas Laundry?"

He ran his hands through his electric-shock Afro. He said nothing. Just nodded affirmatively.

"How about M&M Butchers?"

He raised his arms in front of him, parallel to his shoulders. He flexed and unflexed his fingers. The short sleeves of his dashiki allowed me to see the muscles in his forearm coil and roll as they writhed and snaked upward past his elbow to his bicep. Again, he just nodded.

"And Freedom Maintenance?"

He wasn't sweating exactly, but his wide ebony face was covered by a silvery sheen. He nodded again, slowly.

The ball was once more in my court. "Do you know of any reason why David Turley would list those outfits and tape the list to the outside bottom drawer of his dresser?"

He seemed to be struggling to retain control over himself, to keep the lid on volcanic areas of his personality. Once again, he said nothing. He nodded once more, this time negatively and more slowly than ever.

I couldn't help smiling. He was making me do all the work.

"Man, you' grinnin' lak a mule eatin' briars," he said.

I was grateful for prying some sound from him. "At the top of the list were two initials: "J.H." and "R.J." I figure J.H. is Janus House and R.J. is you."

"Man, you is wilder than a peach-orchard shoat. I got no idee 'tall what you goin' on 'bout."

"Look, a man's missing. I've been hired to find him. I've no idea why he's missing or where he is. I toss his apartment and come up with nothing but a strange list of vendors who do business with Janus House. You handle Janus House's business. Don't you have some idea what it's all about?"

"That all you got, Fletcher? That all you wants to ax me? You got nuffin' mo'? No other questions?"

"Not now I don't."

"'Cause yo'll sound like yo'll got an angle for some

kinda game. You play games with me man and I be all over yo'll lak white on rice. Yo'll play games wif me yo'll just as well give yo' soul to God, cause yo ass is mine." He was glaring malevolently.

I said nothing.

Slowly the fire faded from his eyes. "Well, Mr. Fletcher," he said urbanely in the cultured tone he could apparently turn on and off at will. "It's as much a mystery to me as it is to you."

I finished my drink. "Where do you do your work?" I asked.

"What do you mean?"

"Miss Sprague told me this is your office. I don't even see a desk."

He did his ho-ho laugh again. "Mr. Fletcher, I have more than one kind of job around here. Have you seen the people we treat here?"

"No."

"Well, they're black. If they're not black, they're Hispanic. Whites are few and far between."

"So?"

"So, I serve as a model for the black and Hispanic members. Except for our member therapists our staff is all white except for me—middle-class white. Who else can they identify with? The members both admire and envy me. They know where I come from. I'm just like them. My father worked as a caulker in the shipyards by day and drank himself blind by night. There were eight of us. He never made enough to support us, so he was bitter. He beat us a lot. When I was six he was run over by a train."

"And you learned a great lesson from your father? You didn't want to work like a dog for nothing?"

"That's it, Mr. Fletcher. I became a street hustler. My mother brought us here to New York and tried to support us by domestic work. We needed money. I hustled. But I was a hustler with a difference. I didn't want to go to jail. I hustled when it was safe to hustle. I saved my money, went to college."

"And now you're a success?"

"I'm doing all right." he said mildly. "I've got an education, lots of money in the bank. And I know the right people—the politicians, the businessmen."

"The people here at Janus House, the members, they want you to live like this?"

"That's right, Mr. Fletcher. They like to see a black man who's made it. They're impressed by this kind of a setup. They like flash. Pale, colorless clipping of coupons they can't relate to. They don't like quiet money, they like loud money. As for me, it's better than a poke in the eye with a sharp stick."

"O.K., but I still don't see how you can get any work done here."

"Fletcher, how much work do you think is involved in this job? I don't have to do much. All the work is done by the members. Marianne takes care of the therapy. I don't even come in here full time. I have other interests. I own a couple of bars, a few restaurants, a dry cleaning store. All I do is make sure that I'm getting what I'm entitled to. Around here I just look things over once in a while to make sure things are going smoothly. I write out checks to pay the bills once a week, and that's it. My main role is to let the members see a black man can make it. A desk, I don't need one. If I need a writing surface I use that table over there." He pointed to the coffee table.

"How did you become involved with Janus House?"

"It's mostly just charity work for me. Oh, I get paid. Probably as codirector of Janus House alone I make as much as you do in a year. But it's not my main source of income. This place was established in '67. It got a lot of ink. I read about it, I read about

Marianne, I read about the board of directors. It looked like the usual thing—a bunch of white folks telling the dumb niggers what to do. I went right to the board and gave them my pitch. Told them they needed a black presence here. It doesn't only help with the members, it helps getting government money to run the program."

"How did Marianne Sprague react to all this?"

"She didn't like it. She still doesn't. I don't get the publicity, she does, but I get enough. She doesn't like that either. But our biggest problem is jurisdictional."

"How so?"

"A good example is the new Janus House that's opening in Brooklyn. In my territory—Gamintown. I wanted to make it the mother house. Sprague didn't even want it opened. I also wanted to do something else. You noticed the switchboard downstairs when you came in?"

"Yes."

"Well in the Gamintown Janus House I wanted every member to have a private phone in his own room. Why not? This isn't a jail. It's a question of according to our members the dignity they deserve."

"How did it turn out?"

"I won one, and lost one."

"Which was which?"

"Mr. Fletcher, there will be no switchboard in the Gamintown J.H. In fact, the phones for Gamintown J.H. have already been installed."

"But this place will remain the mother house."

"That was the ruling of the board, but you can rest assured that I will reopen the issue at a later date."

"It seems that your relationship with Miss Sprague is a strained one."

"That's putting it mildly, Mr. Fletcher. She hates me, I hate her. It's that simple."

From what I had seen so far—that wasn't exactly news to me.

"What do you think about her program?" I asked.

"Do you think if we opened up a chain of soup kitchens around the world we'd solve the world's food problems?" He was as relaxed as a sleepwalker now, as unperturbed as a cat on the prowl.

"It doesn't work?"

He grinned—like a mule eating briars. "What do you think, Fletcher? Sure some are cured. Not many, but we probably cure as many as other programs. I'll tell you what the cure for heroin addiction is, Mr. Fletcher. It's not to stick that needle in your arm in the first place. I didn't. I was raised in the same type of environment as our members, but I'm no junkie. There's lots more like me."

"It sounds as though you don't respect them much."

"Respect? That's a funny word, Fletcher. A man gets the respect he demands and deserves. You don't get respect just for being born." He chuckled softly. "You're fuzz, Fletcher, but you almost sound like one of these sorry-ass liberals running on about the problem of race in America."

"I'm smart enough to know that I don't have the solution to that problem."

"That is smart, Fletcher. Do you know why? Because it's an unanswerable problem. The idea of integration is a pious myth, Fletcher. Most Americans, black and white, don't really want it. Not strongly. Therefore, integration, true integration is unrealizable."

"Does the name Nicole Percy mean anything to you?"

His eyes narrowed but he said nothing.

"Luke Stackhouse? Brian Percy?"

"They are the principals of M&M Butchers," he said quietly.

"How about Clyde Lincoln? Pearl Jackson?"

"They are the principals of Atlas Laundry." His reply was even quieter this time.

"Earl Washington?"

"He's partners with Pearl and Nicole in Freedom Maintenance."

"When exactly did you start with Janus House?"

"March 1968. Why?"

"Doesn't it strike you as odd that Atlas, M&M, and Freedom were organized right after that, in April and May of 1968?"

"Odd? Why odd? I told you this place needed a black presence. When I came on board I saw to it that some of the money flowing out of Janus House flowed into the black community. I knew some brothers and sisters who had some money and wanted to go into business. I was in a position to throw some business their way. Is there anything wrong with that?"

"On the face of it, no."

"I hope you don't go around stirring things up, Fletcher. That license you have isn't for life, you know." His voice had taken on a menacing overtone.

"I don't like to be threatened, Jeanette," I said.

"Threatened? You don't know what threatened is, boy. Do you know how much it would cost to hire someone to walk around you with a knife and leave you too short to hang up?"

"Two thousand dollars?"

"Less. A lot less. Does that provide you with food for thought?"

"It would take less than that to provide me with food for thought," I said. "I don't want my gourd stomped."

"On the other hand, someone like me, with my contacts, is in a good position to throw a lot of business to someone like you."

"I can well imagine, but I'm very choosy about the business I handle."

"Sometimes it doesn't pay to be too choosy, Mr. Fletcher."

I thought about the balance in my bank account before I had deposited the $100,000 fee I received for the Parrish case. It had been thinner than the shadow of a starved chicken. "How well I know."

"I would suggest then, Mr. Fletcher, that you keep it in mind," he said before reverting to his down-home accents. "She-e-e-e-e-t, man, you ain't no knothaid. Yo'll just do yo' job an' fin' that missin' chile. I'm sho' sorry that us folks heah at Janus House ain't gonna be able to hep yo'll much, and like that."

I'd gone as far as I could with him for the time being. I stood up and said, "I guess that's all for now, Mr. Jeanette, but we'll be in touch."

"You better think twice before you contact me again, Fletcher. There are people in this town who like nothing better than paying out white folks that insist on harassing brothers. If you do get any smart ideas though, call me at this number."

He scribbled a telephone number on a cocktail napkin and handed it to me.

"I'll do that."

"If you don't want your face eaten you will."

He was the kind who always wanted the last word.

I let him have it.

43

Chapter 7

I took the subway to 96th Street, and picked up my car. I drove down to a parking lot near the World Trade Center and left it there while I got some printouts from World-Wide Information Services.

As usual, no one was in the outer office of World-Wide but Evelyn Perrault, Charley Byers's secretary. No one would be in the inner office but Byers himself. They were the sole work force of World-Wide, a subsidiary of *The Globe*, which on a fee or subscription basis supplied digests from *The Globe*'s information bank of all stories that had appeared in *The Globe* since 1969, and digests of certain stories and articles from other newspapers and magazines since 1970.

"Yes sir, may I help you?" asked Evelyn. The three of us usually engaged in a ritualistic game whenever I showed up at World-Wide. The scenario was always different when we played the game, but the premise was the same: neither Evelyn nor Byers had ever seen me before, while I was there on business that had nothing to do with World-Wide.

"Yes, I'm here about the Martians," I said.

"The Martians, sir," asked Evelyn. "I'm afraid I don't understand."

"This is World-Wide Information Services?"

"Yes."

"Well, I have information that the world should know about."

"I'm afraid, sir, that we don't . . ."

"Important information. Information that every last person on earth should be aware of."

"You see, sir," said Evelyn patiently, "what we do here is supply digest . . ."

"Don't you realize, young lady, that they're coming?"

"Who would that be, sir?"

"Why the Martians, of course," I said, adding a tone of urgency to my voice. "The Martians are coming! The Martians are coming!"

Evelyn stood up from her desk and began to edge nervously toward Charley's door.

"The Martians, sir? The Martians are . . ."

"Coming! Yes, coming! I've been in touch with them."

"In touch with them, sir?" she said more politely than ever. "How did you do that?"

She was a few steps closer to Byers's door. "Radio, of course," I said. "I pick up their transmissions from my fillings."

"Your fillings, sir?"

"Yes, of course. How else could I do it?" I opened my mouth wide and pointed to the fillings in my teeth. "From my dental fillings. I pick up their messages from my dental fillings."

She edged closer to Byers's door. Her hand was on the knob. "Your dental fillings?"

"Where are you going?" I asked sharply. I stepped toward her.

She flung open the door and bolted into the office. I was right behind her. "Mr. Byers," she said, "this man has been in touch with Martians. He says that . . ."

Byers was standing near the left wall of his office with a putter in his hands. About half-a-dozen golf balls were lined up at his feet. Startled by our entrance his hands did a hitch as he followed through on his putt, sending the ball at least a foot wide of the tipped-over wastepaper basket planted against the opposite wall into which he was trying to place the ball. "Damn!" he said, looking at us. "Martians? What's this about Martians?"

"This gentleman says that . . ."

"You are in a position to do a great service for mankind, sir," I interrupted, "I . . ."

"He's been getting messages from Martians, Mr. Byers," wailed Evelyn. "He gets them through his teeth—the fillings in his teeth."

"I see," said Byers. "Very well, Evelyn, I'll handle this." Byers waited until Evelyn closed the door behind her before he turned to me and hissed, "You fool! I told you never to contact me here. Not even by telephone."

"It's all right, Chief," I said apologetically. "She just thinks I'm some kind of nut. She'll never . . ."

"You know our procedures," he said coldly.

"I know, but this is an emergency, Chief."

"The procedures are quite clear on this point. Article 28-A, subsection (d) (3) states, and I quote"—he opened up his desk diary and pretended to read—" 'At *no* time shall a field agent attempt to contact his control except by means of prior approved channels.' *Prior. Approved. Channels.* This is not a prior approved channel."

"I know, Chief, but . . ."

"Let me continue," he snapped. "The penalty for

46

failure to adhere to this procedure is instantaneous dismissal. *Instantaneous dismissal!*"

"But Chief . . ."

"Silence! Stand at attention!"

I stood at attention.

Byers came from around his desk and ripped imaginary epaulets from my shoulders, imaginary stripes from my sleeves, imaginary brass buttons from the front of my coat, and withdrew an imaginary sword from my imaginary scabbard, broke it into two pieces across his knee, and flung the pieces disdainfully over his shoulder.

"But, Chief, this is an emergency. The Martians are really coming."

Byers fell to his knees. As he stumped his way back to his desk, he said, "Don't you think I know that, you fool. Who do you think I am? Why do you think I periodically shrink in size like this?"

"You mean that you . . . ?"

"Exactly," he said, withdrawing a ruler from the middle drawer of his desk. "I am from the vanguard force of Martians. You now know it, and must be eliminated." He drew a bead on me with his ruler, and made a buzzing sound.

I clapped my hand to my heart and staggered backwards, sprawling into a chair, legs extended, arms hanging limply, head lolling over the back of the chair, eyes rolled up in the back of my head.

"Virgil," said Byers, "a few years ago you would have taken a pratfall onto the floor."

"I was younger then," I said. "Besides, the material wasn't worthy of a pratfall."

"You're right. Our routines are getting pretty threadbare. When are we going to grow up, Virgil?"

"I don't know. Some habits are hard to break."

47

When I left World-Wide I had printouts for Marianne Sprague, Robie Jeanette, and Janus House. The computer turned up nothing on Atlas, M&M, or Freedom Maintenance, and nothing on the principals of those outfits.

Chapter 8

I parked at the garage under the Municipal Building and hustled over to Fong's on Mott Street. "Virgil," said Marshall Fong when he saw me standing at the rear of the crowd waiting to be seated, "it's a pleasure to see you. You usually let more time pass between your visits to us."

I had seen him just a few weeks before when I was working on the Parrish case. "If it were a matter of choice, I'd be here every day, Marshall."

He escorted me past the crowd to his private booth near the kitchen. "You sure got a lot of ink on that Parrish case, Virgil," he said.

"You have to admit it was a big story."

"Sure was. And a *big* fee," he said.

"You'll get no argument from me on that."

"I'm sure you earned every penny of it. I'm happy for you. The next best thing to my making money is for my friends to make money. What'll it be today?"

I always overate at Fong's. It had the best Cantonese in the city. I ordered house special soup, stuffed shrimp, sum sut mein, barbecued roast pork, fried chicken with mushrooms, and Mongolian won-ton. As I ate, I read the printouts.

Robie Jeanette had been a councilman and was currently a Brooklyn district leader—the Gamintown district leader. One story claimed that he controlled an empire worth $50 million a year in public funds. He was chairman of School Board 510, with an annual budget of $25 million. He also controlled the Gamintown Poverty Corporation ($2.5 million); as well as the District 600 school board; the Gamintown Neighborhood Manpower Center; three day-care centers; five summer lunch contracts for 65,000 lunches a day; and a nursing home.

To most people, Gamintown looks like Cologne after the firebombing, but for Robie Jeanette it was a paradise. Several stories charged that millions of dollars in federal funds poured into the area had been diverted and skimmed off by Jeanette and his henchmen who controlled the antipoverty apparatus. Jeanette didn't even live in Gamintown. He lived in luxurious splendor in an exclusive bedroom community in Nassau County. He did maintain the obligatory voting address in his satrapy.

Close to two hundred individuals on the payroll of School Board 510 belonged to Jeanette's clubhouse. Fifty-two of the businesses that received contracts from the school board had officers who were campaign contributors to Jeanette's club, his annual dinner, or his club journal.

The Robie Jeanette Day-Care Center at 25 Paxton Street stands right next to Jeanette's clubhouse at 23 Paxton Street. The contractor who built the center was a contributor to Jeanette's club. Jeanette's wife, Nicole, was the executive director of the day-care center. The day-care center was sponsored by an antipoverty agency controlled by Jeanette.

Jeanette's most trusted operatives were given jobs as directors of the various antipoverty programs controlled by Jeanette, and were on the boards of other programs and planning bodies, as well as School Boards 510 and 600.

Jeanette brooked no opposition to his iron control of his empire. People who tried to speak out against him at school board meetings and the like were punched out. In the sixties, before Jeanette had consolidated his power in Gamintown, several of his more vocal opponents disappeared or were murdered. Those who disappeared were never found; the murders were never solved.

In 1969 Jeanette, as chairman of School Board 510, signed a contract with Educational Development Services (EDS) to purchase $850,000 worth of educational materials for use in District 510 schools. Jeanette signed the contract without competitive bidding and without the knowledge and approval of the rest of the school board.

Jeanette signed the contract while he was in Cleveland to speak at a conference organized by EDS. He was hired to speak at the conference for a $5000 fee from EDS's PR firm. The main speaker at the conference was a governor of a midwestern state who had been given a $500 speaking fee. EDS paid airfare and all expenses for Jeanette, his wife, some of Jeanette's school board loyalists, and a few staff members of 510's school board.

Attempts to audit the school boards controlled by Jeanette were unsuccessful because of missing ledgers and accounting records. The audits did reveal certain overexpenditures, and paid vouchers for mysterious junkets to various pleasure spots around the world.

Several of Jeanette's closest colleagues had been indicted and convicted on criminal charges distinct from the governmental activities to which Jeanette was most closely connected. Jeanette himself had never been indicted for anything, but a grand jury had recently been convened to look into his operations.

And so it went, story after story detailing patronage, legal graft, corruption, and personal empire building.

Marianne Sprague's press clippings were almost as colorful as Jeanette's, but there was no hint of scandal associated with her name. She was controversial, and had been embroiled in a number of professional feuds with psychoanalysts, psychiatrists, and therapists concerning the proper treatment of drug addicts.

Both her reputation and that of Janus House were good, and had been enhanced by a number of articles she had written about drug addiction that appeared in professional journals, and by two books by her about Janus House that had become national best sellers.

Her biggest asset seemed to be her talent for enlisting the support of prominent individuals in the arts, politics, and business for her Janus House work. Scarcely a month went by without some mention of her fund-raising activities for Janus House, or an article detailing a verbal fusillade aimed by her at one or another of her professional colleagues who chose a different approach to the treatment of drug addiction than that followed by Janus House.

Some of the stories hinted at a certain tension between Jeanette and Sprague. As he had already explained to me, he had more or less forced himself on Janus House during its first year of operation when it had run into difficulties securing governmental funding for its operations.

An outright war developed between the two of

them in early 1970 when what Jeanette described as "a grass roots rebellion of oppressed brothers sick and tired of domination by whitey" erupted at Janus House. Sprague identified the same incident as "wanton disregard for the physical, psychological and psychic health" of the Janus House members.

According to the accounts, one Everrit Thompson, a Janus House member, either at the instigation of Jeanette, or on his own, organized the other members in an attempt to put total control of the Janus House program into the hands of its members. Whether or not Jeanette was responsible for the insurrection, he joined forces with Thompson and served as the most prominent advocate of the members' takeover. After the takeover, Jeanette said, he would remain as "coordinator" of the activities of the program. After a few weeks the revolt was suppressed, largely due to the pressure exerted by the board of directors who came down firmly on Sprague's side. An uneasy truce was arranged between Sprague and Jeanette, clear lines of responsibility were given to each, and they were both retained as codirectors.

I had exhausted the material contained in the printouts as well as my capacity for taking on any more of Fong's exquisite cuisine. I said good-bye to him, promising to return as soon as possible, and headed for the Bronx. I was more or less at a standstill, but I figured if I poked around enough I'd stir things up and force something to develop.

Chapter 9

IT was the South Bronx. A wasteland. Vast stretches of rubble were all that remained of whole blocks whose buildings had been razed to make way for new housing projects that were never built. Other blocks held nothing but burnt-out tenements and abandoned buildings which offered mean shelter to welfare squatters and served as shooting galleries for junkies.

Crescent Street was better than the rest. The factories and warehouses were old and dilapidated, but they were still standing, and most of them were occupied. I could scarcely decipher the faded lettering that proclaimed the three-story brick structure to be Atlas Laundry. There was plenty of parking space in the cobblestone courtyard. I followed the rickety wooden stairs up three flights to the door marked "Office." There were two desks in the outer office. Behind one sat a middle-aged peroxide blonde typing out invoices. The other desk was empty. In back of the blonde was a door leading to another office. The upper half of the door was pebbled glass. Neatly stenciled on the door in black was: "Mr. Goldberg."

"What do you want?" asked the blonde in a ripe Bronx accent.

Obviously, Atlas Laundry wasn't used to receiving unexpected guests. "I'd like to see Mr. Goldberg, please," I said, handing her my card.

She held it under her nose and scrutinized it as closely as a scholar examining a palimpsest. "A private investigator?" she asked. "Wait here." She scurried from behind her desk and into Goldberg's office, closing the door behind her. In a few moments she reopened the door and ushered me into Goldberg's warren.

He was short, bald, and muscular with intelligent little eyes. "Fletcher? I read about you in the papers. What can I do you for?"

The room was well lit but so small that Goldberg's desk and chair, another chair placed in front of Goldberg's desk, and the single filing cabinet took up most of the space. I decided against sitting in the unoccupied chair. It looked like it hadn't been dusted in over a year.

"I'm looking for a missing person."

"Missing person? *Oi gevalt.* This is a laundry."

"The name of the missing person is David Turley."

"Davids I know plenty. But Turleys? None."

"He's an accountant for Post-McBride."

"We should be so rich we can afford Post-McBride!"

"He recently audited Janus House."

"Janus House I know," said Goldberg proudly. "Lots of customers we got here, Mister Detective. Over five hundred. I know every one. Janus House is kind of small, but they're good. No headaches. They pay on time. But why come here for your missing man, this David Toomey?"

"Turley."

"Whatever. You think this is Missing Persons, maybe?"

I ignored him. "How long has Janus House been your customer?"

"How long, he asks? The first. The first new customer we had when we started."

"When was that?"

"May, 1968."

"Are you an owner of this firm?"

"I should be so lucky," he said.

"Who are the owners?"

"If it's any of your business, it's owned by Luke Stackhouse and Pearl Jackson."

"Where are they?"

"I should know? You think my bosses tell me where they are? I'm lucky if I see them once a year."

"You run the place for them, is that it?"

"I do. And a good job I do of it too. Don't misunderstand. No complaints. They pay me well."

"How did they happen to hire you?"

"They knew me. I'm a good businessman. I used to own a kosher deli in Brooklyn, Gamintown, they live there. You know Gamintown?"

I nodded.

"Then you know that's no place for kosher. Twenty, twenty-five years ago it was a good business, but now . . ." he shrugged eloquently, "now the people in Gamintown they don't eat kosher."

Up until seven or eight years ago there had been a small Jewish community in Gamintown, but it had been overwhelmed by the rising black tide pushing north from central Brooklyn, and it was now overwhelmingly black with a few stray pockets of Hispanics.

"So you had to close up shop. No business?"

"That's putting it mildly," said Goldberg. "I'm a

56

good businessman, but what could I do? I loved the place. My grandfather opened it in 1905. I saw what was happening, but I stayed too long."

"Why did Jackson and Stackhouse hire you?"

"Who knows? Maybe they liked my pickles. I made my own."

I gave him a hard stare.

"O.K., tough guy, I didn't ask. What they knew from running a laundry was nothing. Me? At least I knew how to run a business. They didn't know too many businessmen."

"How did they happen to buy this place?"

"Look, they came to me with a proposition. 'We got some money Mr. Goldberg. We want to invest it, open a business. We don't know from running a business. You do. We put up the money. You run the business. You're through here—they were right, I lost the deli—we'll make a good deal.' They did. I heard the family wanted to sell Atlas. We talked. They gave me a price. I gave them a price. We dickered. I gave them a price. They gave me a price. We talked some more. We agreed. Business!"

"Where did Stackhouse and Jackson get the money to open this place?"

"It was a good price. It was cheap at twice the price."

"But where'd they get the money?"

"I should ask such questions? Let me tell you something, Mr. Detective. In polite company people don't ask such questions. I don't ask such questions. They tell me they have X amount of dollars to invest, I should call them a liar? No. I believe them. When time comes to put up the money, they got."

"You say you know all your customers. How much business do you do with Janus House?"

I was testing his knowledge. He welcomed the

challenge. He smiled like a cat. "How close you want it?"

"The nearest thousand?"

"I can do better. I can give you nearest hundred. Say $9,900 last year."

"How did you get the account?"

"How did I get? How did I get? I got it from Robie Jeanette. He runs Janus House."

"You know him?"

"Everyone in Gamintown knows Robie Jeanette. And why shouldn't he throw some business our way? Luke Stackhouse is his cousin. Pearl Jackson's his sister. What's wrong with helping out your relatives?"

"Nothing at all. How sure are you about the amount of business you do with Janus House?"

"Greta!" yelled Goldberg.

"Yes, Mr. Goldberg!" she yelled back.

"Get the invoices for Janus House for 1975!"

Greta didn't reply, but in a few moments she returned and handed Goldberg a manila folder.

"Come over here, Mr. Detective, and I'll show you something," said Goldberg.

I joined him behind the desk. He opened up the folder and pointed to its contents. "What's that, Mr. Detective?"

I picked up an invoice from Atlas Laundry dated February 5, 1975. It billed Janus House $919.85 for the month of January 1975. The invoice was marked: "Paid Feb. 12, 1975."

"It's our bill to Janus House for the month of January 1975," said Goldberg. "We bill them monthly." He went through each invoice and entered the amount indicated on the Janus House check into a calculator that was on his desk. There were twelve checks, one for each month in 1975. The total for 1975 came to $9,918.25. "Well, Mr. Detective, does Goldberg know

his business, or does Goldberg know his business?"
His smile was wider than a sumo wrestler's hips.

"Goldberg knows his business," I replied.

It was a good exit line.

Chapter 10

M&M Butchers and Freedom Maintenance stood right next to each other on 125th Street off Broadway. I had to park about a block away from their entrances. I felt a thousand eyes on me as I walked toward the stores. Some were curious, some were hostile, all were suspicious. None were friendly.

There were no customers in the butcher shop. Two white-aproned black men stood behind the counter. They watched cautiously as I entered, but neither of them said anything.

I stretched my face into its most winning smile and said, "Good afternoon. The name's Virgil Fletcher. Robie . . . Robie Jeanette said you might be able to help me."

They relaxed a little when I said that. The older man spoke first. He was tall and slim, coffee-colored, with high cheekbones and a neat pencil mustache. His silvery gray hair was gassed. "How's that?"

"I'm a private detective," I said, handing him my card. "I've been hired to find a missing person. He's an accountant. He worked on Janus House's books and records. You know, to make sure everything was

O.K. for the government. His name's David Turley. Have either of you heard of him?"

They both nodded negatively.

"He's only been missing a few days. He finished his work at Janus House last week. He never gave either of you a call or anything?"

The younger man was tall, and round as a barrel. "No one call' from Janus House 'ceptin' to order meat," he said in a rumbling big man's voice. He started hacking savagely at a hunk of beef with a cleaver.

"Are you the owner?" I asked him.

"No." He grunted as he slammed the cleaver into a bone.

"Then it must be you," I said to the older man.

"No," he said politely. "I'm the manager."

"Is the owner around? Maybe he spoke to Dave."

"Miss Percy owns this shop, sir. She's not here. She lives on the Island."

"Maybe he talked to her. Can I have her telephone number?"

The older man used a stubby pencil to write the number on a scrap of butcher paper, and handed the paper to me. I thanked them and left. It was a Nassau County number.

It was almost five. I walked past Freedom Maintenance to a telephone booth on the corner and dialed the number the butcher had given me. "Jeanette residence," said a softly cultured voice at the other end of the line. I hung up. I called Janus House and asked for Jeanette. He wasn't there. I spoke to Sprague instead. I asked her to stay until I arrived. She agreed.

"Well, Mr. Fletcher, why all the mystery?" asked Marianne Sprague.

"No mystery," I said. "I'd just like to look at some of your records for 1975."

"Records? What kind of records?"

"Billings by vendors and payments by Janus House."

"But Mr. Fletcher, that's not my area."

"I know, but surely you must know where the records are kept?"

"I do but I'd prefer that you deal with Mr. Jeanette on this."

"Do you know where I can reach him?"

"No I don't, but I don't see why you have to have them this minute."

"Miss Sprague, I'm looking for a missing person. Virtually the last bit of work he did was for Janus House. There's a good chance that the files I want to look at will give me a lead about where to find him."

"I don't see . . . oh, very well, Mr. Fletcher," she said resignedly. "I know where the records are."

They were in a filing cabinet outside Jeanette's office.

The filing cabinet had been locked. In order to open it she had to use a key that was one of at least fifty that hung from a ring held by a nail driven into the wall in back of the bar in Jeanette's office. While I looked for the records Sprague said, "You can use my office if you need work space. I have to go to a fund-raiser." She placed her hand on my arm. "You're a very unusual person, do you know that?"

"My mother thought so," I said. "Why do you think so?"

"I look for dedication and commitment in people, Mr. Fletcher. It's a quality that's much rarer than you might think. I can see that you have it. Your first name is Virgil, isn't it?"

"Yes."

"Do you mind if I call you Virgil?"

"Not at all."

"Please call me Marianne."

"I'd be happy to."

She gestured dramatically with her right arm, waving it in a circular motion, and rolling her head from side to side. She clinked and clanked as she did so. "I'm so dedicated to all this," she said. "It leaves me so little time for a personal life. I wouldn't mind if we got to know each other better." She blinked her eyes rapidly and flashed a coy knowing smile.

She projected a sensuality that surprised me. The kind that could grow on you if you let it. "I'm sure we will," I said.

"Why don't you give me a call tomorrow?"

She might not have much time for a personal life, but it seemed she liked to have firm control of whatever time was available. "I'll do that."

She left.

In the filing cabinet I found folders with billings for Atlas Laundry, M&M Butchers, and Freedom Maintenance and brought them to the desk of Marianne Sprague. Her In and Out boxes were empty, but the surface of the desk was covered by a designer's building layout. I glanced through the floor plans casually. They were for the Brooklyn Janus House, the one in Gamintown that was due to open soon. It was as Jeanette said—no switchboard, and telephones everywhere.

The Atlas Laundry file contained more than the twelve bills Goldberg had shown me. Three times as many. One for every week of the year. Attached to the stack of bills was a calculator tape that indicated that the total amount of the invoices was $49,849.74. The invoices that Goldberg showed me had only amounted to $9,918.25—a difference of almost $40,000.

Oh boy! This thing was beginning to smell worse than one of the Sheepshead Bay party boats on its way back from a day of fishing when the mackerel were running.

I separated the bills Goldberg had shown me from the others. It was easy to do. The handwriting on Goldberg's bills was different from the handwriting on the other bills. Goldberg's bills were all dated on the first Wednesday of each month. The other bills were dated on the other Wednesdays of the month. Goldberg had not submitted these other bills.

Payment for all of the Atlas Laundry bills had been made by checks drawn on the Janus House account at the Manhattan Trust Company. The checks had all been signed by Jeanette. The Janus House checks made out to Atlas Laundry for Goldberg's bills had been endorsed by Goldberg and deposited to the Atlas Laundry account at the Bronx Merchant's Bank; the Janus House checks made out to Atlas Laundry for the other bills had been endorsed by Pearl Jackson and deposited to the Atlas Laundry account at the Gamintown Bank.

That made sense. Goldberg hadn't submitted the bills, so he didn't deposit the checks. Why should he? He'd never seen them, unless he was part of the scam. I doubted that. I didn't know if he was honest or not. How many honest people do you know? I did know he was too smart for something like this. If he got involved in fraud he'd do something a little bit more sophisticated than this. This was outrageous. It was also imaginative, ballsy, and probably not that easy to detect. It had a certain flare to it that I suspected could be attributed to Jeanette. There was no question he was in it up to his neck.

M&M Butchers and Freedom Maintenance told the same story: twelve bills for each concern paid by

Janus House checks and deposited to their accounts at Harlem banks close to their locations; forty other bills for each organization paid by Janus House checks deposited to their accounts at the Gamintown Bank.

I did not recognize the endorsements on the checks deposited to the Harlem banks. They were probably signed by Goldberg's counterparts—the guys who actually ran the businesses.

I recognized the names of the endorsements on the checks deposited in the Gamintown Bank. Nicole Percy endorsed the checks made out to M&M Butchers. According to the information I got when I called the County Clerk's office from the phone on Garth Lambert's desk at Post-McBride, she was one of the principals of M&M. Pearl Jackson, one of the principals of Freedom Maintenance, had endorsed the checks made out to that outfit.

It was the same deal as Atlas Laundry: legitimate bills submitted by the managers, paid for by Janus House, and deposited to local banks; phony bills submitted by the principals, paid for by Janus House, and deposited to Gamintown banks.

Added to the forty grand paid for phony bills at Atlas Laundry, the total amount of phony bills paid for by Janus House came to $105,672. The legitimate billings from all three organizations came to only $73,019. It was Jeanette's handiwork all right. Who else would be so bold as to actually submit more in phony claims than were submitted in legitimate claims?

I used Sprague's phone to call him at the number he had given me earlier in the day.

He was unhappy.

"I thought we had an understanding, Mr. Fletcher," he said.

"Maybe it was a misunderstanding."

"You've been going around stirring things up. I don't like that."

"I might have stirred things up more than you think."

"How's that?"

"I'm here at Janus House now. I've gone over the billings for Atlas Laundry, M&M Butchers, and Freedom Maintenance."

He sighed. "How'd you get your hands on them?" he asked. "That bitch, Marianne?"

"Right."

"She's a difficult woman, Fletcher. She can't hold up her end of an agreement. She thinks she can nail me."

"It looks like you have a lot of explaining to do. We better get together and talk."

"You don't know shit from shinola, boy," growled Jeanette in his hush puppy accent.

"Shinola comes in a can," I said.

"All right, Mr. Fletcher," he said in his normal speaking voice, "we'll meet."

"When?"

"I think you agree it should be as soon as possible?"

"Yes."

"How about tonight?"

"It's O.K. with me," I said. "Where?"

"Yo'll 'fraida Gamintown when the sun go down?" He was back to his cornpone routine.

"I'm afraid of a lot of things. I don't enjoy the prospect. Why can't you get down here?"

"I can't. Not tonight. I've got business to take care of, Janus House business. That new house I told you about right here in Gamintown. I made a deal with the landlord about what I wanted him to do before I buy. He's a whitey slumlord. I'm supposed to meet

66

him there tonight, at ten o'clock. Suppose you come by tonight, before he arrives. Say nine o'clock."

Nine o'clock in Brooklyn. In Gamintown, the heart of Jeanette's empire. "You're not getting any ideas, are you, Mr. Jeanette?" I asked. At least at nine there'd still be some light.

"Ideas? What kind of ideas?"

"Well, like getting rid of me."

"Mr. Fletcher, I am a respectable businessman and civic leader," he said. "I would never entertain such a notion. Besides, I'm not stupid. You've got your hands on something now that . . . ah . . . might cause me some slight embarrassment. You have time to conceal it. To pass it on. To do any number of things. Why, boy, you safer ri' 'chere in Gamintown than in yo' own bed."

"I'm glad to hear that."

"It's true, Mr. Fletcher, we're both reasonable men. We have to talk."

"O.K., but let me ask you one thing."

"What's that?"

"How did you get a slumlord to meet you in Gamintown after dark?"

He chuckled softly. "Business is business, Mr. Fletcher. He's got a white elephant he wants to unload. I want it. We talked. He gave me a price. I gave him a price. We dickered. I gave him a price. He gave me a price. Tonight we talk some more. Business!" Jeanette was marvelous. He had just given an almost perfect imitation of Goldberg. Phrasing, diction, voice—all were virtually flawless.

I wrote down his directions to the Gamintown address, copied all the material in the files I had just read, returned the files to the cabinet, put the photo copies in a manila envelope I found in the mail room, addressed the envelope to myself at my mail drop, ran the envelope through the stamp machine, and left.

I used the door at the end of the hallway to leave the building. As I suspected, the door opened on a flight of stairs that led to a back entrance to the house. The entrance was an alley that led to the street. I didn't run into anyone.

On the corner, I mailed the letter.

Chapter 11

THE house was a three-story brownstone. It stood on a
street that was cut in two by the elevated line. A pink
Cadillac Coupe de Ville was parked in front of the
house. Two men were in it. I parked in back of the
Cadillac. When I got out of my car, the two men got
out of the Cadillac.

One of them was Jeanette. The other was muscle.
Big. I'll tell you how big: big enough to block out the
sun. That's big.

"Well, Mr. Fletcher, it's a pleasure to see you again,
sir. Shake hands with Luke Stackhouse, one of my
business associates."

Luke Stackhouse of M&M Butchers. He looked like
a butcher, but not the kind you see behind the coun-
ters in shops. He was the kind I run into in dark al-
leys, or lonely piers, or anywhere or anytime when I
least felt like dealing with King Kong. He was no
more a businessman than I was a ballerina. His shoulders were as wide as the Holland Tunnel, and his
grip was as strong as an anaconda's. I'm tall, but this
guy could eat pie off the top of my head. A nasty scar
wormed from one ear across his cheek and disap-

peared where his collar met his neck. It stood out like a white caterpillar on a black sheet. He bent down and peered intently into my face with eyes as mean as those of a ferret.

"He's just trying to remember your face, Mr. Fletcher," said Jeanette mildly. "He hates not remembering people he's supposed to remember."

"My pleasure, Mr. Stackhouse," I said. "Meat's your line I believe?"

Stackhouse said nothing.

"Wait here, Luke. Mr. Fletcher and I are going to talk inside." Jeanette reached into the outside pocket of his evening clothes and extracted a ring of keys that I assumed was the duplicate of the one that had been hanging from a nail in back of the bar at the Manhattan Janus House.

He opened the door and fumbled for a light switch on the inside wall of the house. He found it and turned it on. A bright light in the high ceiling illuminated the entrance foyer. In the center of the foyer was a body which was reflected in the mirrors that covered each wall of the foyer.

The body was the right size to be Turley, but I couldn't tell from the face. It was covered with congealed blood.

Jeanette closed the door and leaned against it. His chin was down around his knees. His widened eyes made two perfect circles. "Lordy! Lordy!" he exclaimed.

I stepped over to the body and looked at the inside of the pinky of the right hand. It had a scar. Chantal Montez had told me her brother had a scar in the same place.

"Do you know who that is, Fletcher?"

"I think it's David Turley." I withdrew a wallet from the inside pocket of the corpse's jacket. The driver's license was David Turley's. I showed it to Jeanette.

"Ah feel so weak ah couldn't pull a greasy string out'n a cat's ear." He heaved a great sigh, took a few deep breaths, and thrusting his hands deep into his pockets, paced back and forth from one end of the foyer to the other, head bowed in thought.

As he paced, I examined the body more closely. One bullet had hit it just above the nose. Three rings of dried blood stained the front of the body's shirt and jacket. In the center of the rings were holes.

I searched the body, taking care to disturb it as little as possible. There was eighteen cents in change, three subway tokens, a set of keys in a black leather case, a wallet with twenty-six dollars in it, two pens, a pocket calculator, and a special leather container that held business cards. Besides the money and the driver's license, the wallet held Turley's social security card and several credit cards. There were some pictures of his sister and three pictures of comely young women. Nothing was written on any of the pictures.

I started preparing in my mind different ways of telling Chantal Montez that I had found her brother. Dead. Murdered. None of them sounded good. There's no good way to tell anyone that someone they love is dead. When the dead person has been murdered it's even harder. "You better call the cops," I told Jeanette.

He stopped. "That's only one of several unpleasant alternatives available to me, Mr. Fletcher. I'm not responsible for this," he said pointing to the body. "But I know a setup when I see one. I could flee. That's my worst alternative. It would make it seem like I'm guilty. I could dispose of the body, but that would mean disposing of you. If I did that I'd have to retrieve that list from Turley's apartment. Even then I'd have to worry about what you did with that stuff you just turned up at Janus House. Yes, I'm going to call the cops, but first I'd like to retain your services."

From the distance the clackity-clack of an approaching subway train could be heard. "For what purpose?"

"To find out who murdered David Turley." He raised his voice so that I could hear him over the noise of the train.

"I already have a client." I had to pitch my voice even higher than his so he could hear me.

"You've done what David Turley's sister hired you to do. You've found him." He was shouting now. It was the only way I could hear him.

"That's true, but I think she'll want me to do more than that," I shouted back.

He cupped his hand around his mouth and yelled in my ear: "So what's wrong with having two clients who want you to do the same thing. You'll just be getting paid twice for doing the same thing."

The train rocketed by, roaring across the tracks of the elevated in front of the building. I didn't even attempt to reply until the noise of the train faded enough to allow me to speak in something approaching a normal conversational tone. It seemed to take a long time. "I can't do that," I finally said.

"You're some straight arrow, Fletcher." He opened the door. "Stack! Hey, Stack!" he shouted. The door of the Cadillac flew open and Stackhouse rolled out, landing on his feet gracefully in a catlike crouch before he bounded across the sidewalk toward the path that led to the house. In his right hand he held a .38.

"Whoa! Slow down, Stack!"

Stackhouse skidded to a halt about ten paces from the entrance to the house. He stashed his weapon in a shoulder holster, and waited for instructions from Jeanette. He was glaring at me.

"Get rid of the piece, Stack. We got a body on our hands. This place will be crawling with cops in a little while. And call you-know-who and tell him what happened."

Stackhouse looked at him uncomprehendingly for a moment.

"Go on now, Stack. Do like I say. Be sure to get rid of that piece."

Stackhouse turned around and glided toward the car. It was amazing to see such a big man move so easily. The Cadillac took off with squealing tires and must have hit fifty before it reached a gas station that stood one hundred yards down the road. It braked with another shriek from the tires and pulled off the road, finally coming to rest before the gas station's office. Before I closed the door, I saw Stackhouse gesticulate to the attendant, reach over the counter to pick up the phone, and dial.

"Why is David Turley's body here?" I asked Jeanette as I dialed 911. I used a phone that was on the floor near the entrance to the room on the right.

"There's only one reason, Fletcher. I'm being framed."

"Who by?"

"I don't know. I have lots of friends. I also have lots of enemies."

"Who but you could have brought Turley's body here?"

"I don't know."

"Let's check this place out," I said. "Fast." The cops would arrive at any moment. I covered the whole first floor. All the windows were barred and locked; the door to the rear entrance was locked. The door opened on a rear driveway that led directly to the street parallel to the one which the building faced. When we finished our patrol of the first floor I told him, "You'll be needing a good criminal lawyer."

Jeanette was calm. Outside of the shock that struck him when we discovered the body, he had been in complete control of himself. "Don't I know it. Look, Mr. Fletcher, everything I've ever done, I was prepared to take the weight. I did everything I could to protect myself, but I had to take chances too. When you start with nothing, you can't end up with something without taking chances. I've fended off investigations of my activities in the past. There are a variety of ways of doing that, you know."

I knew. Deals. Bribes. Threats. Anything, even murder, to call off the wolves.

"But I didn't kid myself that I could do it forever," he went on. "Oh, I hoped to, and I knew with just a little luck I would. But if I didn't . . . if I didn't . . . well, I've got plenty put away. I've got lots of legitimate income. I can hire the best attorneys. I figured if it came, I'd fight it. There's not much they could get me for but white-collar crime. So what? A fine, a suspended sentence, or maybe a year or two in jail. With time off for good behavior less than that. I can take the weight." Lost in his thoughts for a moment, he stopped.

"The penalty for murder is heavier than you want to carry," I said.

"I don't want to go to jail and come out an old man."

"Or not come out at all."

"Thanks for reminding me."

"So who wants to get you so bad that they'd set you up like this?"

"As I've already said, I've got lots of enemies."

"Names, Mr. Jeanette?"

"Why should you care? Why should I answer your questions? You've refused to work for me."

"But I do want to find Turley's killer. You say you're innocent. O.K., help me find the real murderer."

"Look, Mr. Fletcher, you already know too much about me. But you don't really know anything about my operation. That stuff at Janus House? Small potatoes! That just helps me take care of some of my friends and relatives, like Stack. That's nothing, Mr. Fletcher. With my connections the *most* I could get out of that would be a fine and a suspended sentence. But my other activities? You want names? Forget it, honky . . . wait, I'll give you a name . . . one name . . . Marianne Sprague."

I stared at him incredulously.

"You don't like that, do you?" He chuckled softly. "Marianne Sprague. Yeah, that bitch hates me all right. But, don't worry, it's not that easy. She doesn't have the stomach for something like this." He pointed to Turley's body.

"Are you sure?"

"Well, she might have the stomach, but if she wanted to set me up she would have done it a long time ago, not now. Now we have a good working relationship going. I leave her alone if she leaves me alone. She leaves me alone if I leave her alone. We leave each other alone."

"Turley's been missing since about noon on Friday. I've seen quite a few stiffs in my time. I'd say he's been dead since sometime Friday afternoon, or early Friday evening. Can you account for your time during that period?"

"I can account for it all right, but I don't know if I want to."

"You'll have to."

"Well, let's just say that my activities on Friday were not the kind of activities I'd like the cops to know about."

The door opened and Stackhouse entered.

"Leave it open, Stack. We don't want some trigger-happy fuzz blowing holes in it."

"Or in us," I said.

In the distance we could hear the insistent claxons of several squad cars. The cops arrived with squealing tires and flashing lights. They arrived virtually simultaneously. There were three squad cars. Cops didn't like to arrive on the scene of a crime with one squad car in Gamintown.

Chapter 12

LT. Enrico Escalero was the commander of the Brooklyn Homicide Zone that included Gamintown in its territory. I gave him my statement in his office in a Brooklyn precinct house. He gave me nothing but the time of Turley's death. According to the M.E. he had been shot three times between 2 and 5 p.m. at the Gamintown Janus House. Death was instantaneous.

When I asked him, Escalero didn't put up too much fuss before he agreed to allow me to break the news of her brother's death to Chantal Montez. I didn't want her finding out about it from a radio or TV news flash. I used his office phone.

"Oh, Virgil," she said when I reached her, "you've found him, haven't you? I knew you would."

I took a deep breath. The easiest way for both of us would be for me to just lay it on her head. I did. "Yes, I've found him. I'm sorry, Chantal, he's dead."

"Oh, God!" she wailed. "How? Why?"

Escalero's back was turned to me, but I knew he was listening closely to my end of the conversation. "He was murdered, Chantal."

"What! But . . . but who, Virgil? Who would want to kill Dave? He didn't have an enemy in the world."

"I don't know," I said.

Perhaps a minute went by before she spoke again. All I could hear was her breathing, heavy and labored. "Virgil?"

"Yes?"

"I want you to find the murderer."

"Look, Chantal, I'll be over there as soon as possible. I'm almost done here." I held my hand over the mouth of the receiver. "Isn't that right, Rick?" I said to Escalero's back. He made no sign to indicate that he heard me.

"Promise me you'll find the killer, Virgil," pleaded Chantal.

"We'll talk about it when I get there," I said.

"All right, Virgil," she said. "Please hurry. Good-bye."

"Good-bye, Chantal."

Escalero turned to face me after I hung up.

"I hope you're not getting ideas, Virgil," he said. His sharp brown eyes probed mine.

"What kind of ideas, Rick?"

"You know, about working on this case. You've done your job. You found David Turley. Now it's a job for the police." He rubbed the huge beak of his nose with his left hand.

"She wants me to keep working on it, Rick."

"The department frowns on that kind of thing, Virgil." His wide mouth was frozen into a half-smile as enigmatic as the Mona Lisa's.

"I know, but as a private citizen Chantal Montez has a right to hire me to investigate her brother's murder. As a private citizen I have a right to accept that employment."

Escalero's face was creased and tired. "O.K., Virgil.

I've made my point. But stop and think: Jeanette is just about boxed in; it's not going to take us long to nail him for this."

"You think he's guilty then?"

"He certainly has the motive. It all adds up. One," he said, holding up his bony index finger in front of his swarthy face, "Jeanette sets up these partnerships for his friends and relatives."

"What are the relationships exactly?"

"Nicole Percy is his wife's maiden name. Pearl Jackson is the married name of his sister, Pearl Jeanette. Brian Percy is his brother-in-law. Luke Stackhouse is his cousin. Lincoln and Washington are old friends and confederates of his, going back to the early days." He kept his index finger in front of his face. "Two." He held up the next finger. "Turley doesn't like the way the billings from these outfits look. Different handwriting on the different sets of invoices, different billing patterns, different endorsements on the payment checks, which were deposited in different accounts at different banks. Three." Up shot the next finger. "Turley maybe gets copies of the partnership papers from the County Clerk, or maybe he doesn't. But he does show Jeanette what he's got and asks for money."

"C'mon, Rick. Turley was no blackmailer."

"Four," Escalero went on, holding up his pinky, "Jeanette doesn't stand still for it, and knocks off Turley."

"And leads me to the body?"

"Why not? It confuses things and makes him maybe look innocent."

"Look, he could have had him killed and had the body deposited someplace where it would never be found."

"Well, he didn't. He killed him in a moment of

79

rage, or he panicked and made mistakes under the threat of exposure."

"Jeanette's not the type to fly into a rage. As far as exposure goes, that stuff between Janus House and those partnerships he set up was nothing. Do you think he'd serve more than a year at most for it?"

"No."

"So why should he murder to cover it up?"

"People do funny things under stress, Virgil. Maybe he dreaded exposure."

"You keep scratching after maybes. Can't you do any better, Rick?"

"You sound like his lawyer."

"He's got a better one than me." I had seen Earl Cosgrove outside Escalero's office talking to the A.D.A. Earl Cosgrove: short, chunky, eyes flashing, square white hands as thick as snowmobile mittens, cutting shapes in the air with eloquent gestures. Earl Cosgrove, the city's, and possibly the country's most brilliant criminal lawyer. "Let's assume he did have a motive, did he have the opportunity?" I asked.

"I don't know yet, but I will."

"How the hell did Jeanette lure Turley to a deserted house in Gamintown?"

"I don't know. Probably the pretext was that he would be paid off. He got you to go there, didn't he?"

"Where was Jeanette Friday afternoon and evening?"

"I don't know that yet."

"Rick, you've got some case. To nail a guy like Jeanette everything has to be airtight. Your case has more holes in it than the Jets' defensive line. Think of the connections this guy's got. He has his own clubhouse. He virtually runs two school boards. He's into all kinds of community corporation and antipov-

80

erty business. He's got friends who can really put the heat on. Had any yet?"

"Not yet. It's too soon. I was hoping I could wrap . . ."

"Wrap it up before he mobilizes his support? That's a pretty faint hope, isn't it?"

"Look, Virgil, I just do my job the best way I know how. I don't always win. Jeanette's the best suspect, the only suspect, we have. Until something better comes along I'm going to try to nail him." He was frowning deeply. It made his thick bushy eyebrows appear as a single broad line over his eyes. "Heat? I don't get heat on something like this. The guys he has for friends don't bother with someone like me. They go right to the top."

"The D.C.?"

"At least," said Escalero.

Deputy Chief Stonebreaker was in charge of the Brooklyn Detective Area. I'd never met him but I didn't like his reputation: an uptight cop of the old school, rigid, inflexible, impatient with the legal restrictions imposed by the Miranda and Escobedo decisions. "Have you heard from Stonebreaker yet?" I asked.

Before Escalero could reply Stonebreaker entered the office. I recognized him from newspaper pictures that had appeared in the past, and from several press conferences he had held to announce big breaks in cases he had worked on. His scrawny, ravaged face and long nose made him look as lean and hungry as a starving wolf. "Rick, we've got all kinds of problems . . . who's this?" he asked when he saw me. His voice was a fretsaw. I didn't like it. I didn't like him.

"This is Virgil Fletcher, a private investigator," said Escalero.

"Fletcher, I've heard about you," said Stonebreaker,

rubbing his forehead vigorously. "You've done your duty as a citizen, Fletcher. Now I want you off the case." He slapped his sides. "Understand?" He thumped his chest. "Permanently." He crashed through his speech as though he was involved in a competition to determine the Fast Talking Championship of America.

"I'm afraid you're not the one who will make that decision, Chief."

"What? What? What?" Stonebreaker asked. "Do you know who I am, Fletcher? I said out! I mean out!" he roared, throwing up his arms. "What is it with this guy, Rick?" he asked, his voice dropping to a whisper.

Escalero just shrugged.

"What is it with you, Fletcher?" said Stonebreaker with a sneer. "Do you like trouble? Do you want trouble?" He sounded like a man at the end of his tether with a world whose absurdity is fathomless.

"I don't like it. I don't want it," I said. "But I won't allow myself and my client to be buffaloed by some egomaniacal cop."

"What? What?" His high forehead framed by his scraggly gray curls was suddenly a washboard. His face leaned close to mine but his eyes were on some faraway spot in space. His hollow cheeks converged on his pale pursed lips. "Buffaloed?" He turned toward Escalero, and asked, "Is this guy a friend of yours, Rick? Well, you better tell him," he went on without waiting for Escalero's reply, "that this is Brooklyn, not Manhattan. We play hardball here. Tell him, Rick!"

Stonebreaker walked out of the office, slamming the door behind him. I could see his shadow through the pebbled glass of the door. He was waiting for Rick to tell me.

"Well, Lieutenant?" I asked him mildly.

"Look, Virgil, don't mess with Stonebreaker. If you do you'll be sorry. If he gets on your case he never lets up. He'll wait twenty years if he has to, but he'll get you."

"I'm disappointed in you, Rick."

"Don't be disappointed. Just listen."

"My client wants me to find out who killed her brother."

"I know," he said.

"I'm going to do it, you know."

"Take her case?"

"Find her brother's murderer."

"C'mon-n-n-n!" groaned Escalero in that drawn out nasal objection peculiar to native New Yorkers.

"Thanks for the advice anyway, Rick."

Stonebreaker glared at me as I left Escalero's office. Don't ask me why I did it. "Hey, Chief," I said.

"What?"

"A chicken ain't nothin' but a bird."

I had never heard the expression before. I had no idea what it meant. It sounded like one of Jeanette's down-homeisms. But I was glad I said it. The puzzled frown on Stonebreaker's face made it worthwhile. Someday I would grow up. But it would be hard with guys, cops, like Stonebreaker around.

Chapter 13

CHANTAL Montez had not so much mastered age as transcended time. Just a few weeks before, her lover Robert Parrish had been murdered. Less than two hours earlier I had told her of her brother's death. Any other woman of her age would have been a wrinkled shell after receiving two such heavy blows in quick succession.

She wasn't. Her smile when she greeted me, although sad, was womanly and ravishing. Her eyes with their giant pupils were tender, intense, luminous. Her pale skin was fine and transparent.

"Virgil, I won't rest until they've found the man who's done this terrible thing," she said. She looked and may have been as vulnerable as a butterfly, but her spirit was diamond-hard.

We were in a room in her suite that I had not seen before. It had a darkly-paneled wall, a cocoa rug and a tree-trunk coffee table. A small gray cat on the windowsill was flicking a red rose with his tail. "The police think they've got the man who did it."

"Who is he?"

"His name's Robie Jeanette. Did your brother ever mention him?"

"No."

"He's the codirector of Janus House, a drug rehab program. He's also the overlord of Gamintown. He has a lock on the public monies that flow into Gamintown."

"What's Gamintown? Where is it?"

"It might be the most blighted area in the city; it's certainly one of the poorest areas in Brooklyn."

"What is this man's connection with David?"

"Post-McBride audits the books of Janus House once a year on a charity basis. The guy who audited the books this year reported to David. He was fired before he could handle the closing conference with Jeanette. As the codirector of Janus House, Jeanette was responsible for paying the bills for Janus House and maintaining their books and records. David handled the closing conference. In the closing conference the auditors go over the results of their audit with the people who were audited."

"That list you found in David's apartment, J.H. stands for Janus House? R.J. for Robie Jeanette?"

"Yes."

"How about Atlas Laundry and the other two businesses?"

"They're partnerships. The partners are friends or relatives of Jeanette. They all did business with Janus House. They submitted phony bills to Jeanette who paid them out of Janus House funds."

"And David discovered this?"

"That's what the police think."

"And David threatened to expose this Jeanette?"

"The cops think he was trying to blackmail Jeanette."

"Virgil, that's absurd! David would never become

involved in something so shabby. He was much too fine a young man for that. You don't think it's true, do you?"

"I don't think that Jeanette would be too worried about exposure of his Janus House activities. A good criminal lawyer could handle it easily. He might have been worried that exposure of what he was doing at Janus House would lead to an investigation of his other activities. I don't think Jeanette would have qualms about murder, but I think he's too smart to do it in such a way that he's the most likely suspect."

"Then you agree that David wasn't involved in some blackmail scheme?"

"Yes," It was a lie. I am always objective about such things. I didn't *think* he was, but I didn't *know* it. Not knowing it, I couldn't agree that he wasn't involved, but I wasn't going to tell her that. I was going to do everything I could to prove that he wasn't involved.

"You will find his murderer, Virgil? You will clear his name? It may seem silly to you, but he was so good, I don't want his memory to be soiled with something like this."

"I'll find his murderer, Chantal. It's not silly to want to clear his name."

"Oh, Virgil," she said, drawing a great racking sigh. "I'm so . . ."

She fell against me, burying her face in my chest and let go. Deep wrenching sobs shuddered through her body, and after a while her tears soaked through my shirt to the skin. I held her head against my chest with my left hand and patted her awkwardly on her back and shoulders with my right. "There, there," I said softly. "Everything will be all right. It's all right, baby, let it all out."

She cried until she had no tears left. She leaned all her weight against me and said betwen hiccups, "I'm so . . . sorry . . . Virgil . . . it's just that . . . I have no one now." With her head pressed tightly against my chest, her voice came out muffled and faraway.

I picked her up and carried her to her bedroom. I pulled back the covers of her bed, put her down, and covered her. Her dry eyes were bloodshot and swollen, unblinking.

"You need rest," I said. "Do you have anything to help you sleep?"

"In the bathroom. Medicine chest."

It was Nembutal. I gave her the dosage prescribed. I held my hand on her brow, and said, "Close your eyes. Sleep."

"Stay here with me, Virgil. I'm afraid and lonely." It was the voice of a frightened child.

"I will. You go to sleep now." I drew a chair close to the bed and held her hand until she was in a deep sleep.

There was an alarm clock on her night table. I set it for seven and took it with me to the room adjoining hers. I took off my tie, jacket, and shoes, and squeezed onto the largest piece of furniture in the room, a high-backed couch. I slept fitfully and at 6:45 gave up trying to do even that. I left a note for Chantal telling her I would be in touch with her, and headed up to my Riverside Drive apartment. On the way I bought the papers. Turley's murder made the headlines, but there was nothing about Jeanette's scam involving Atlas Laundry, M&M Butchers, and Freedom Maintenance. When I got to the apartment I shaved and showered. I skipped breakfast.

The case didn't make any sense to me. David Turley wasn't the type to blackmail, but if he wasn't, what was he doing with that list of vendors on the underside of his bedroom dresser's bottom drawer? Assuming that he did know about these outfits and their relationship to Jeanette, how did he find out? He didn't do the audit himself. The audit was done by Garth Lambert, the aspirin freak. All David did was handle the closing conference. At least, that's what Avildsen, the Post-McBride manager said. So if David knew or suspected something it must have come from Lambert. I'd find out about that when I talked to Lambert.

I went back to the list of vendors. Assuming Turley was blackmailing Jeanette, why a list? There were no details on it, just names and initials. Surely Turley's memory wasn't so bad that he had to write down so little lest he forget it. Another thing, why was the list typed? If your memory was so poor that you did have to prepare a list, isn't it more likely that you would write down the information by hand? Of course, someone else could have prepared the list and given it to Turley.

Another thing—if Turley was blackmailing, what was he using as proof to threaten Jeanette? If he didn't have the kind of evidence I had sent to myself at my mail drop yesterday, he was running the risk of giving Jeanette time to destroy evidence or to muddy the waters that it might be impossible to prove he was involved in hanky-panky. Hell, even with the stuff I had Jeanette might never serve a day in jail. But if Turley did have proof of wrongdoing, where was it? All my toss of his apartment had turned up was the list.

And how did Turley wind up in a deserted house in Gamintown? If he was blackmailing Jeanette, wouldn't he have been more cautious than to have met him on his own turf? Then again, if he wasn't blackmailing him, what was he doing there at all?

I was getting nowhere. I stopped thinking about it. I'd have to get more information before I'd be willing to think about it some more.

Chapter 14

I was going to look up Garth Lambert, the guy whom David Turley fired, but before I left the apartment the phone rang.

"Hello?"

It was Jeanette.

"I've got something that might interest you," he said. "Can you get over here?"

"Where are you?"

"I'm in Gamintown, You know, the new Janus House. I want to see how some renovations are coming."

"Like a new boiler?"

Jeanette chuckled softly. "That's one of them."

"And Freedom Maintenance has the job?"

"Sho' 'nuff. Why not? They do good work."

Jeanette was going to brazen it out until the bitter end. "O.K. I'll leave now."

"Right on, brother."

The cabbie didn't like the idea of a trip to Gamintown. Even the edge of Gamintown. He started to protest, but I silenced him with a cold stare. My tough-guy stare. It worked. Sometimes it didn't. Tough guys don't scare many people anymore. There are too many other things to be afraid of.

The place didn't look as sinister in daylight. It had a fresh, scrubbed quality. The squeaky-clean windows sparkled in the sun, and whatever wood showed on the outside had been freshly painted. It was almost cheerful.

The signs identifying it as a crime scene and warning not to trespass had been posted. A uniformed patrolman stood on the sidewalk in front of the house with the bored, faraway look common to anyone doing guard duty. The cop was milk-skinned, big and burly. He had the face of a ruined choirboy. "You Fletcher?" he asked.

"Uh-huh."

"Mr. Jeanette is expecting you." Obviously Jeanette had no problem handling the man on the beat. "Got some I.D.?"

I walked the path to the front door and opened it. There were dark stains on the floor where Turley's body had been yesterday. The mirrored walls of the entrance foyer reflected the interiors of the two rooms adjoining it. The house was empty and silent. In the distance I heard the rapidly approaching clatter of a subway train. It grew louder and louder, drowning out all other noise. It took a while for it to pass. It must be hell to listen to that racket all night. "Jeanette!" I yelled when it fell silent once more. "Jeanette!"

"Fletcher! That you, old buddy?" It was Jeanette. He leaned over a wooden bannister of the staircase on the floor above me. He was resplendent in a custom-made three-piece white-on-white suit made of raw silk. His shirt was navy blue, his tie a bold yellow. He wore a flashing diamond pinky ring on his right hand and the ring finger of his left hand was adorned by another ring whose stone looked like a sapphire. "Come on up."

I trudged up to the second floor. He grasped my hand and wrapped his left arm over my shoulders. "Right this way."

He led me down the hall to the right past freshly painted rooms empty of furniture. All of the rooms had phones. The door to the last room was closed. Jeanette leaned close to me and peered at me with slightly glazed eyes. His breath reeked of alcohol. Ten in the morning, and the guy was hitting the bottle. He opened the door and stepped into the room ahead of me, stumbling slightly as he did so. He was drunk. Not 'knee-walkin' drunk, but drunk. "Looky, heah, Fletcher, what you think 'bout it?"

The room was a revelation. It made his room at the Manhattan Janus House look like a hovel. It was opulent, if garish. There were four windows in the room. Hanging plants framed one of the windows facing the El. The other was banked with plants and bordered at the top with shirred white shades. The south window's shade was linen and cotton fabrics strung on wire; it served as a backdrop for vertical rows of oiled wooden beads, strung irregularly, which ran the whole length of the window. The north window was obscured by a piece of clear glass suspended in front of it depicting the nude torso of a lissome black woman in profile. The walls were mirrored. Jeanette had a jones for mirrored walls. A maroon rug with a nap as thick as a pimp's roll covered the floor and the furniture was plush. A bar was placed in front of the two west windows. Shelves in back of the bar ran up to the ceiling and held an assortment of booze that would stock the watering hole of a convention hotel for a week.

Another train passed, its racket making it impossible for us to hear each other. Jeanette strolled behind the bar. The bottles were arranged according to the variety of the drink. All the bourbons were together; all the Irish; all the Scotch; all the tequila; all the cherry liqueurs; all the chocolate liqueurs; all the . . . but you get the idea. There was no kind of booze he didn't have. In dumbshow he offered me a drink, pointing to each section in turn. He started with the bourbon. I shook my head no. He went to the Irish, and then the Scotch. I turned down each in turn. He shrugged, and looked at me quizzically.

I figured I might as well have something—he'd badger me until I did—so I mimicked opening the door of a refrigerator, extracting a bottle, opening it, and chug-a-lugging it. I was hot, dry, and thirsty.

Jeanette pointed to a round panel in back of the bar that was decorated with coasters advertising beer, ale, and stout from all over the world. The coasters were arranged alphabetically.

I pointed to the Ringnes coaster.

Jeanette bent over and disappeared from sight. When he reappeared his right hand held, opened, the familiar squat green bottle, frosted with beads of moisture. He gave it to me and poured maybe two fingers of a white liquid from a bottle whose label faced him, into a tumbler that stood before him on the bar. He produced a lime from some place underneath the bar, cut off a slice, balled his right hand into a one-potato, two-potato fist, sprinkled some salt from a cellar that stood on the bar onto the area just in back of the thumb and index finger of his right hand, raised the tumbler to me in a toast, licked off the salt, drained the tumbler, bit into the lime, and licked his lips appreciatively. He threw the lime wedge into a mammoth ashtray that was already crowded with other wedges. Tequila.

I shuddered just a bit. On one horrible night years ago in Tijuana I had consumed at least a quart of the stuff, ingratiating myself with a wooden-legged bargirl who had eventually provided me with the information I needed to find a kidnapper I was tracking down.

He got life.

I got sick. Very sick. Sick enough so that I would never forget the thick kerosene taste of the fifth-rate tequila I had forced myself to imbibe.

I returned Jeanette's salute with my bottle, raised it to my lips, tilted back my head, and let it drain down my throat as fast as it could empty. It was an old trick. A matter of releasing a catch in back of the throat so that you wouldn't choke and gag on the liquid. When I was fourteen I spent two months during July and August with my brother Caesar who was stationed at a base in Florida in the middle of a mangrove swamp. That's where I learned it—from the locals. My spending money was heavily allocated to Cokes during the learning period, and Caesar didn't appreciate the darkly stained shirts that were the evidence of my unsuccessful attempts to master the arcane feat, but after a few weeks I could do it as well as the locals. Better. As I grew older I learned how to do it with beer. At one time I thought it was quite an impressive stunt.

Jeanette thought it still was. The sound of the departing train had ceased, allowing him to say incredulously, "Ain't you got no stopper back there?"

"It's just a trick," I said modestly.

"You'll have to show me sometime." He sounded like a man without a care in the world, a man with plenty of time to enjoy life. Certainly not like a man facing a lot of years, perhaps the rest of his life, behind bars for murder.

"I'd be glad to," I said.

We shared for a moment the silent communion of men who like to drink before he said, "I suppose you're wondering why I asked you to come?"

His voice was crisp and businesslike. All trace of his chitlins and hog-maws accent was gone, as was the faint slur of a man who had more than a bit too much to drink. I wondered how much of that tequila he had actually drunk. It couldn't have been that much—not if he was able to snap back like this. Maybe he was the type who liked the idea of getting drunk but not the reality. Some guys are like that. "That's a good supposition," I said.

"Mr. Fletcher, I want to hire you."

"I thought we went all over this yesterday."

"I don't give up easily, Mr. Fletcher. I'll triple, quadruple your usual fee. Anything you say. The rats are abandoning the sinking ship. The cops aren't trying to find out who killed Turley, they're trying to pin the thing on me."

"You're wasting your time," I said.

"Mr. Fletcher, I can be very persuasive. Just give me ten minutes to tell you why you should take the job. But let's relax first. Stack's going to call me any minute. I left him a message at the Manhattan Janus House to call me on the phone down the hall. Private business that doesn't concern you. When he calls you, stay here. When you know too much, your life sometimes loses its value for other people. Understand?"

I nodded.

"Let me tell you something, Fletcher. I love this life. Wouldn't trade it for anything. Make some money, throw everything on the next shot, blow it, start over, I love it. I've been up half-a-dozen times, been down about the same. I was close to some big ones before I got my Gamintown setup, but close only counts in horseshoes."

It sounded like an exit speech. A ringing phone interrupted it. He strode across the room without another word as the noisy rumble of another train approached. He closed the door behind him.

It wasn't an exit speech.

It was an epitaph.

Chapter 15

THE train rocketed past the house, rattling the windows, and the glasses on the shelf behind the bar. It wasn't going to be easy for the members to conduct their group therapy and encounter sessions in this atmosphere. At least not during rush hour.

I waited for Jeanette.

And waited.

I looked at my watch.

10:25.

I waited some more.

The house was so quiet it was like being underwater.

I looked at my watch again.

10:35. At least twenty minutes since Jeanette had left to answer the phone.

I decided to look for him.

An acrid odor raised goose bumps on my body when I opened the door. I turned left and strode down the hall. I didn't bother to check the rooms I had already seen when Jeanette led me to his den. The ringing phone he had gone to answer sounded further away than the ones in those rooms.

It was. It was the phone on a packing crate holding a desk in the alcove to the left of the stairs Like the rest of the phones in the house, it had a push-button dial.

That's where I found Jeanette.

Behind the crate.

Dead.

His torso was collapsed over the crate. His right cheek rested in a dark, sticky puddle of blood. His vacant eyes stared straight ahead. His left arm hung limply. His curled upright arm rested on the desk next to his head. In his half-open right hand was a piece. A .38.

The receiver of the phone was in its cradle. It rang again and I picked it up. The button on the bridge did not light up.

"Robie?"

"This is Fletcher. Who's this?"

"Stackhouse. Put Robie on."

I told him as quickly as possible I couldn't, and why. I wanted to get the cops there fast, but wanted to check the house out first. He hung up immediately. I wondered why he had called back.

I didn't touch Jeanette except to feel his wrist. Warm, but no pulse. There was no doubt he was dead. I looked for a note. There was none. There wasn't always a note.

I didn't like the setup. Jeanette wasn't the type to kill himself. I decided to make a quick tour of the house. The room in back of the chair in which Jeanette's corpse rested was empty, save for another packing crate holding a desk, another chair in back of the desk, and a phone on the desk. The room looked like it was going to be used as an office. The phone number coincided with one of the numbers for the phone on the desk over which Jeanette's body was slumped.

I opened a door in the north wall of the room. It was the twin of the room I had just been in. It too contained a desk-shaped packing case and a chair. The number of the phone on top of the packing case coincided with the other number for the phone in the hall.

It looked as though the two rooms were to be used as offices, with a secretary shared by the occupants of both. Her duties would include screening incoming calls.

The rest of the rooms on the second floor were like the ones I had already seen in the east wing of the house. So were those on the third and fourth floors: relatively small and narrow, and empty save for a telephone on the floor.

I started my tour of the first floor at the rear of the house. The back door was locked. The rest of the first floor contained a kitchen, a large room off the kitchen that would probably be the dining room, another room, even larger, which could serve as a recreation area, and three other smaller rooms. The house looked empty. I didn't check the basement.

To call the cops I used the phone in the hall where we had found Turley's body. I went out to the sidewalk and broke the news to the patrolman.

He didn't like it one bit. "Holy shit!" he exclaimed. "Mr. Jeanette? He shot himself?" His ass was in a sling. Neither Jeanette nor I had any business being there, not while the crime scene posters were up, not while he guarded the house. It was his job to keep us out, and he hadn't.

"I didn't say that. I said it looks like he did."

He brushed past me and ran into the house. I followed him at a walk. When I got back to the hall he was standing at the top of the stairs looking down at me.

"Did you touch anything?" he asked.

"I didn't get my license at Korvettes," I said.

"Holy shit," he repeated. "Mr. Jeanette." He looked stunned as he trudged back down the stairs. "Mr. Jeanette. I can't believe it."

That didn't mean it wasn't true.

Chapter 16

"FLETCHER, you're a real bird of ill omen, aren't you?" It was Stonebreaker. His voice annoyed me as much as ever. *He* annoyed me as much as ever. His red-rimmed sunken eyes were like two chips of coal pushed into a snowman's face.

We were standing in the room to the right of the house's entrance hallway. The M.E. was upstairs. The forensic lab boys were waiting for him to finish. "A gooney bird or an albatross?" I asked. Stonebreaker had been on my case since he arrived, and I didn't like it.

"C'mon, Virgil," said Escalero, "take it easy."

The guy from the Medical Examiner's office, Dr. Friedman, entered the room. He was tall and heavyset, bald, and had a bushy black beard. His black eyes were bright and shiny, and his voice was pompous, slow, as if he held it up for his own admiration. "It looks like suicide, Chief. It's a contact wound. It's been distended from gas pressure. The eyes are exophthalmic. That's from gas pressure too."

"Suicides are easy to fake," said Stonebreaker. "Can you rule out homicide?"

"Oh course not, but it's not likely, unless he was passed out drunk or asleep when it happened," said Friedman.

"How about if he was drunk but awake?" asked Escalero.

"Sure. That's possible. It depends on how far gone he was. Hell, it's even possible he was cold sober and wide awake. It's just not likely. I don't see how someone could just walk up and . . ."

"Let me worry about seeing how," snapped Stonebreaker. He had a way of charming everyone.

"I see no reason to call it anything but suicide," said Friedman in a dignified tone. "Our blood sample will tell us how much he drank. You probably won't get prints. Too much blood."

"I'll worry about the prints." Stonebreaker was sure pleasant. "So you say it's suicide?"

"I said it looks that way. My formal opinion will be given after the autopsy."

"Thanks. Thanks a lot, Doc." Poor Escalero had to pick up the pieces after Stonebreaker. "We'll be in touch." He put his arm around Friedman's shoulder and escorted him to the front door.

"You're a real diplomat, Chief," I said to Stonebreaker.

"I'm getting tired of your face, Fletcher," he said.

"I'll leave then."

He grabbed my arm. I shrugged him off. "Wait a minute. I'm not through with you yet. I'll tell you when you can go, wise guy. I could book you right now."

"For what?"

"Trespassing into a prohibited area."

"Sure. Why not arrest me for that double-parking violation I got a month ago. I haven't paid the ticket yet."

Stonebreaker scowled. "How about murder, Fletcher? You're the only one that was on the premises when Jeanette was killed."

"Are you going to throw out the suicide theory?" Not likely. Suicide wrapped up two cases for him: Jeanette's and Turley's.

"Why should I tell you what I'm going to do?" Stonebreaker's face twisted into something resembling a smile. A tight smile. He wasn't smiling though. His eyes were as mean as a junkyard dog's.

"What is this, twenty questions?" I couldn't help it. I had to drive Stonebreaker to the brink, or over it. It was so easy to do, and I enjoyed it so much. He was one type of cop I could do without. Not that there were many I could do with. You can't last long on the Force very easily without having an authoritarian personality, and I don't like authoritarian personalities. They substitute commands for thought. Anarchy is closer to my style. That's not good, not bad, it's just my style.

Stonebreaker bit his lip so hard that he drew blood. Not much, but I did see a faint smudge right under where his lip should be. "You say Jeanette was drunk. How much did he have to drink?"

His face was now so close our noses almost touched. His breath was fetid. I turned my head away and waved my hand in front of my face. "Phew! Didn't you ever hear of mouthwash?"

His body became as tense as a rabbit's under the gun. His hand shot out to grab my lapels. I caught them before they reached me. "Look, but don't touch," I said. I didn't care if he put his hands on me. In fact, I wanted him to. I wanted him to do more than that—take a punch at me. But not alone, only in front of witnesses. Say what you will, cops can't get away with that kind of stuff anymore, not if you knew

103

what to do about it. If he took a punch at me in front of a witness, then he'd be off my case. For good. I released him.

He shook himself and screamed, "How much! How much!"

To get him madder, I kept my voice pitched in conversational tones. "How do I know? His breath stank from hooch. He wasn't that steady. But it could have been an act. He snapped out of it when Stackhouse called."

"Don't give me speeches. Fletcher. Just answer yes or no. Tell me again why you came here."

I said nothing.

"Well?"

"I'm afraid I can't answer that with a yes or no."

"You know what I mean, wise guy. Just answer my questions."

Stonebreaker had cracked a lot of cases. It wasn't because he was smart. He was a bastard. That was probably why. Bastards can often drive men to do more and better work than they normally do. But that only worked for routine stuff, production stuff. This wasn't routine. Stonebreaker was in over his head, and we both knew it. He didn't like that, which was one of the reasons he didn't like me. I had given him others. There wasn't much he could do about it though, except harass me a little and make things difficult. I liked him as much as he liked me. Less. There wasn't much I could do about it. Except harass him a little and make things difficult. "Yes," I said.

"Yes? What do you mean 'Yes'?"

"Yes, I'll answer your questions."

"That wasn't my question."

"What was?"

He paused for a moment. Maybe he forgot his question. "Why did you come here?"

"Jeanette."

"Jeanette what?"

"Asked me."

"But why?"

"I told you why. Because Jeanette asked me."

"No! No! No! No! No!" he yelled. "I know that. Why did he ask you?"

"I don't know."

"Then why did you come?"

"Because he asked me." Escalero had reentered the room. "Rick," I said, "do all Brooklyn cops work up these Abbott and Costello routines?"

Escalero patted my arm. "Take it easy, Virgil. Easy." He turned to Stonebreaker. "Let's take him to the precinct and get his statement, Chief. What do you say?"

Stonebreaker's rice-colored face was in flames. "*You*. Not me. *You* get his statement, Lieutenant." He looked at me. "I told you I don't like your face. Make sure I don't see it again. I want this guy straightened out, Lieutenant."

"Are you saying I'm crooked?"

"You better button your lip, or you won't have one," he said.

"You don't have one now," I said. It was true. His lips were nonexistent; his mouth was a razor's edge.

His right came out of left field. A real sucker punch. Except for turning my head slightly to take it on my cheek I didn't try to avoid it. He was about four inches shorter than me. Maybe six foot. He couldn't have weighed much more than one-fifty, which gave me seventy pounds on him. I figured he had no punch. I was right. It couldn't have broken a pane of glass.

"Oh, my god!" Escalero shouted, stepping between us. He held Stonebreaker by both arms. "C'mon, Chief, get out of here." He was unhappy.

105

I wasn't. I had Stonebreaker where I wanted him.

Escalero tried to hustle him out the door.

I blocked their path. "Wait a minute, Rick," I said. Stonebreaker's eyes were vacant. "I want you to straighten *this* guy out. I want him off my case." Poor Escalero. First Stonebreaker, now me, using him as an interlocutor.

"O.K., Virgil, O.K. Anything you say."

I stepped aside. They went into the hall and closed the front door behind them. In a few minutes Escalero returned. "You shouldn't have done that, Virgil," he said.

"What? Put my face in front of his fist?"

"You know what I mean."

"I hate to think about what he does to people who don't know the ropes."

Escalero shuddered slightly. "Don't ask," he said.

Stonebreaker was off my case.

For good.

Chapter 17

GARTH Lambert was an unprepossessing young man. His painfully asymmetrical face was made uglier by a huge cleft in his upper lip. His hair and handshake reminded me of a Raggedy Andy doll. His eyes were dull with sleeplessness. It was 12:30. After my incident with Stonebreaker, Escalero had taken my statement in record time.

He stared blankly at my card. "A private detective? Why do you want to see me? I haven't slept all night. I want to hit the sack."

"It's about David Turley."

"Dave? What about him?"

"He was found dead last night. He was murdered. His sister has hired me to find the murderer."

"Please come in," he said. His eyes weren't quite as dull now.

His apartment was cramped and poorly lit. The furniture looked like it had been bought at an auction for a transient hotel that had gone out of business. It spoke eloquently of Lambert's loneliness.

I sat in the cleanest-looking chair in the living room. The room was hot and stuffy, without air conditioning. Lambert sat opposite me. He was dressed in a scruffy bathrobe. His bare legs were pale and scrawny. "I don't know if I can help you, Mr. Fletcher," he said, lighting a cigarette. "David was my boss but I hardly knew him. We didn't exactly travel in the same circles." He sucked on his cigarette as though he were desperate to get the smoke in his lungs. When he inhaled all he could, he didn't exhale immediately, but held the smoke as long as possible. When he finally did exhale, nothing came out but a thin wisp of blue smoke. The rest was retained by his body. He was the type who'd continue to smoke through a hole in his throat after his cancerous larynx was removed.

"He did fire you, didn't he?"

"Oh, sure, but there were no hard feelings. Post-McBride wasn't for me, I wasn't for Post-McBride. Let's face it, I don't need those headaches."

I remembered the mammoth bottle containing a single aspirin that I had found in his desk drawer. "When were you fired?"

"My last day will be two weeks on Friday."

"So you were fired on June 25th?"

"Right."

"What was the last job you were on?"

"I did an audit of one of those drug rehab places. Janus House, it's called."

"Anything unusual about the audit?"

"No. Nothing at all."

"You normally did your audits on the premises of the organization being audited, didn't you?"

"Always."

"How often would you normally see Dave?"

"Too often." He held up his hand. "Don't misunderstand! Nothing against him. It was just a reflection on my ability. The senior accountants usually don't spend much time at the audit site."

"But with you Turley did."

He nodded morosely. "I didn't make mistakes. I didn't have questions. I was just . . . well, too slow." He savagely stabbed out his butt in an overflowing ashtray that stood on the coffee table in front of him. The index and middle fingers of his right hand were stained yellow from nicotine.

"Too slow?"

"Too slow for Dave. He was a crazy gung-ho guy. I did things as fast as most of the other juniors at Post-McBride, but too slow for Dave."

"Didn't you resent that?"

"Sure, but what was I going to do, punch him in the mouth? He was twice as big as me. I tried to talk to him about it, but he wouldn't listen. All he wanted was results."

"How often was Robie Jeanette around?"

"He'd come in once a week. How do you know about Jeanette?"

I ignored his question. "How long would he stay?"

"A couple of hours."

"What did you think of his setup?"

"Are you kidding? Do you know what he makes?"

"No."

"$35,000 a year. $35,000 to come in and sign checks, pinch ass, and booze it up."

"You don't approve?"

"Hell, no. Taxpayers' money helps to support that outfit, right?"

"You tell me."

"Sure it does."

"Did you do anything about it?"

"Like what?" He lit another cigarette.

"Talk to Dave, for instance."

"Yes. He told me to MYOB, mind my own business. He said it was a charity account that received special attention from Mr. Post. David didn't want to hear about any problems. He just wanted things wrapped up as quickly as possible."

"Did you ever hear of Atlas Laundry?"

"I don't think so." He lit another cigarette and went through his baby sucking routine again. "Are they hiring accountants?"

"How about M&M Butchers?"

"You're beginning to jog my memory."

"Freedom Maintenance?"

"They're vendors, aren't they? Janus House vendors?"

"You tell me."

"Yes, I remember them now."

"Did you notice anything unusual about their billings?"

"No, should I have? You must remember one thing, Mr. Fletcher: neither Mr. Post nor David wanted anything but a quick job at Janus House. They wanted the books audited enough so that the program's financial statements could be certified."

Smoke began to curl from the ashtray. His butts were on fire. He picked up the heaping ashtray and scurried out of the room. From somewhere in the back of the apartment I heard the sound of a flushing toilet. He returned in a moment with the ashtray. It was stained black and yellow, but there were no butts in it. He lit yet another cigarette.

"Do you know who owned those three outfits?"

"Should I?"

"It was Robie Jeanette."

He raised his eyebrows, and nodded his head slightly. "I . . . see . . . now," he said. "What was the scam?"

110

I told him.

"Not exactly sophisticated," he said. "It was effective though. But I wonder why . . . ?" He broke off.

"You wonder why what?"

"Oh, nothing," he said quickly. "I was just thinking maybe we should have picked it up. But of course we couldn't have."

I didn't care to hear why he thought it couldn't have been picked up by the Post-McBride auditors. Wally Post could do that himself. I had a hunch Lambert had been thinking about something else. "That's all you were wondering about?"

"Sure. What else could there be?"

His face looked innocent. It's not hard to look innocent, particularly if you're making an effort not to look dumb. I let it go. "What did your audit focus on?" I asked.

"Big items—rent, depreciation, salaries."

"Salaries? What about Jeanette? Wasn't that a no-show job?"

"Yes, but he was paid from a special Janus House account that involved no government money."

"What kind of an account?"

"It was the money Janus House raised each year in their semiannual drive for contributions."

I remembered those drives: hordes of Janus House members on busy street corners buttonholing passers-by and aggressively dunning them to buy raffle tickets for automobiles; rock concerts at Felt Forum; and mass mailings asking for contributions. "In other words, they could use this money as they saw fit."

"Right."

"How large was this account?"

"Not too large. After deducting expenses, maybe $100,000."

"What was it used for besides Jeanette's salary?"

"Oh, junkets to conferences for Marianne Sprague and other staff members. Educational expenses for staff members."

"The government funds wouldn't cover these expenses?"

"They'd probably cover the expenses for some of the conferences if they dealt specifically with drug addiction. They'd also cover educational expenses if the courses were related to the work of Janus House. This account was for conferences and educational expenses that couldn't be covered by government funds."

"Then Jeanette's salary wasn't coming from governmental funds, was it?"

"No."

"But before you said . . ."

"I know what I said, Mr. Fletcher. What difference does it make where the money came from? I have to work for my money. You work for yours. Why should someone get a free ride just because he's black? Besides, these programs are b.s."

"Why do you say that?"

"I think Marianne Sprague's on pills."

"Pills? What kind of pills?"

"Uppers. I know the look. Did you ever look at pro football teams on TV during the playoffs?"

"Sure."

"Those close-ups before the beginning of the game? Guys pounding and banging on each other? Jumping up and down? Especially guys on the special teams, the suicide squads. Ever see close-ups of their faces? They don't pan in often, but when they do . . . zonked out . . . eyeballs like test patterns . . . foaming at the mouth. Ever see that?"

"On occasion."

"Well I've seen Marianne Sprague look like that."

It was interesting, but I didn't know if it was pertinent. "How about the billings from vendors? Did you check any of them through?"

"Yes."

"How?"

"By sampling some bills and seeing that the bills were paid and deposited to the account of the vendor."

"That's all?"

"No. In some cases we asked the vendors to confirm their billings and payments."

"How did you do that?"

"By writing to the principals of the vendor firms."

Neat. Even if Lambert or other auditors before him had checked out the partnerships set up by Jeanette they wouldn't have contacted Goldberg or the others who actually ran the organizations. They would contact the owners, Jeanette's friends and relatives. Naturally, their responses would coincide with the information contained in the Janus House files. "When David Turley came to see you at Janus House how long would he stay?"

Lambert lit another cigarette, and voraciously dragged on it. He really enjoyed them. I felt a passing desire for one myself. I had quit cold turkey three months before, and still had an occasional yen to pollute my bloodstream with nicotine. "With me?" he said. "Not long. He'd hock me for a while and spend the rest of the time with Marianne Sprague."

"With Marianne Sprague? I didn't know he had any contact with her."

"Are you kidding? They knew each other pretty well."

"How well?"

Lambert's pale eyes avoided mine. "I don't know. Well."

113

"How did they meet?"

"Dave audited the Janus House books a few years ago."

"When?"

"I think it was '72."

"Just exactly what was their relationship? Did they sleep together?"

"I think so. Did you ever meet Dave?"

"No."

"Well, he was the kind of guy women line up for. And Marianne Sprague . . . she has some reputation."

"What kind of a reputation?"

"Well, the scuttlebutt at Post-McBride was that she spent more time on her back than on her feet." He lit another cigarette from the butt of the one he had just lit.

"You mean that the various auditors of Post-McBride who did the books at Janus House . . ."

"Yes. But not me," he said ruefully. "I'm the kind women run away from. Maybe if I hadn't been fired she would have gotten around to me."

"Can you give me names of people at Post-McBride who enjoyed her favors?"

"Well, Joel Friedman did the books last year. He said she 'fucked like a mink.' Those were his words. He said she was unbelievable in bed. Sensational, he said. Joel's a senior accountant now. He said that Marty O'Garrity had her also. Marty did the books the year before Joel. I don't know about that. Marty's still with Post-McBride."

"You're telling me that Marianne Sprague systematically took the Post-McBride auditors home with her?"

"Did I say take home with her?"

"O.K., not take home. The auditors took her to their apartments."

114

"I didn't say that either."

"You mean right at Janus House? Where?"

"Have you ever seen Jeanette's office?"

"Oh, no . . . you're kidding?"

"That's what the story is."

That was funny. A symbolic dumping on Jeanette. I wondered if he knew or suspected what was going on. "And that's where she and David Turley . . . ?"

"That might of happened a couple of times with them while I was there. I think it did. But they disappeared a lot too."

"Turley was a special case?"

"It looked like that to me."

"How often did Turley show up while you were there?"

"Let's put it this way, Mr. Fletcher. He was there much more than was ncessary."

"How often?"

"I'd say nine or ten times."

"In how short a period?"

"About three-and-one-half weeks," he blurted out bitterly. "I probably wouldn't have been fired if he didn't have to justify spending so much time with me."

"You didn't like him much, did you?"

"He was a bastard!"

"Can you tell me how you spent last Friday?"

"I can tell you how I spent the whole Fourth of July weekend, Mr. Fletcher. Right here in this apartment smoking dope and watching the boob-tube."

"Did you see anyone? Any friends?"

"No. I don't have many friends. Besides, after you've been fired you don't feel like socializing." He nervously shoved another cigarette into his mouth, and reached for the lighter on the coffee table.

"You've already got one going," I said pointing to

115

the partially smoked cigarette resting in the ashtray. He ground it out and lit the fresh one, breathing the smoke down into the pit of his stomach.

"Have you found a new job?"

"I've had a couple of interviews. I've got a couple more lined up. I better get one. I'm running out of bread. I don't want to move back to Jersey with my folks."

"Have you ever been to Gamintown?" I asked.

"Good God, no!" he replied.

"Do you know anything about Janus House opening another facility in Gamintown?"

"I saw the floor plans in the file. It has lots of telephones."

"How about Sprague and Jeanette? How did they get along?"

"Scuttlebutt was, they didn't."

"Scuttlebutt from where?"

"Oh, Post-McBride, and also what I picked up at Janus House."

"What kind of scuttlebutt?"

"Oh, nothing unusual."

"I'll be the judge of that."

"The most interesting item concerns Billy Jefferson. She's Jeanette's secretary. Some secretary," he said sourly.

I remembered her vividly—the regal looking woman with the coffee-colored skin, the oriental eyes and the body like a brick pagoda, who was draped all over Jeanette when I first met him. "What about her?"

"She comes in with Jeanette once a week. For that she gets paid fifteen thou a year." He shook his head unbelievingly.

"Is she paid from the special account? The one they set up with the charitable contributions they receive?"

"Yes."

116

"You didn't tell me about that before."

"I forgot. Look, Mr. Fletcher, I was just fired a few weeks ago. I've got other things on my mind."

"What about Billy Jefferson?" I asked.

"Oh, Jeanette and Sprague had a big fight about her a few months ago. Sprague said it was a disgrace to have her on salary. Jeanette told her to bug off."

"Sprague told Jeanette . . . What about her own activities?"

"Maybe she thinks she's more discreet," Lambert said mildly.

"Who told you this story?"

"Florence."

"Who's Florence?"

"She's one of the members. She's been operating the switchboard. She knows most of what goes on there. She and I . . . well . . . you know. Women just had to look at David Turley and they'd spread their legs. Me, I have to settle for a black junkie who's been poked more times than a punchboard." He didn't like himself much. Or anyone else for that matter.

"What was the other gossip?"

"Oh, just that they didn't like each other—Jeanette and Sprague—they've had a lot of arguments."

"Do the members know about her sexual activities?"

"I didn't hear anything. Things are quiet in that wing. No one's ever there but Sprague, Jefferson, Jeanette, Sprague's secretary, Mrs. Dowd, visiting dignitaries, and Post-McBride accountants for a once-a-year three- or four-week visit. Mrs. Dowd has been with Sprague for years. She's completely devoted to her. She wouldn't say anything."

"Any talk about her getting sexually involved with members?"

"Not that I heard of."

117

"By the way, did you hear that Jeanette snuffed himself this morning?"

"Jeanette? No. Why?"

"You seem surprised."

"He wasn't the type."

"I didn't think he was either. Any ideas?"

"No."

That's what he said, but he looked like he was thinking hard. It was a mess. According to Lambert, Sprague was a pill-popping nympho who bedded down David Turley and hated Jeanette. Lambert himself admitted that he hated Turley.

Things were getting more complicated.

I didn't like it.

Chapter 18

WALLY Post liked it less than I did. He had heard about the suicide but not about the fraud. The country squire of Post-McBride, elegantly bedecked in a baggy brown tweed suit, puffed furiously on his churchwarden and paced the floor as I summed up for him what I had learned so far.

"You mean that Jeanette was paying for phantom bills submitted by concerns owned by his friends and relatives?" he asked.

"That's right," I said.

"And that David Turley knew about this and tried to blackmail Jeanette?"

"That's *not* what I said. That's what the police think. Can you tell me why Jeanette's phantom billings weren't picked up in your audits?" If he really didn't know, it wasn't surprising. Apparently media reports had not mentioned it yet. The cops were keeping the lid on still.

"I most certainly can," he said. He strode to the bookcase on the wall, searched for a moment, and pulled down a volume. "Note the title and the source," he said, holding the spine for me to look at.

The spine read: *Codification of Statements and Auditing Procedures.* It had been published by the American Institute of Certified Public Accountants.

Post leafed through the book until he found the passage he was looking for. He read it aloud to me: ". . . the ordinary examination incident to the issuance of an opinion respecting financial statements is not designed and cannot be relied upon to disclose defalcations and other similar irregularities."

"O.K., I understand. Your audit was only designed to certify the financial statement, right?" I told you accounting wasn't a science.

"Yes, just as Mr. Avildsen explained yesterday. Nevertheless, I must confess I don't like this. I don't like it at all."

"There's other things you'll probably like less."

He stopped in his tracks and peered at me from underneath his bushy brows. "Honestly, Mr. Fletcher, I've had enough bad news for one day."

I got up from my chair and started to walk out. "If you're not interested in trying to find the murderer of one of your employees and in learning about what goes on under the roof of Janus House," I said, "I'm wasting my time." I wasn't serious. I knew that I could count on squeezing out as much cooperation from him as I needed. I was just softening him up. I wanted more than reluctant cooperation. Reluctant cooperation meant I would have to spend time and energy where it really wasn't needed. I wanted active cooperation.

"Wait a minute, wait a minute, Mr. Fletcher. Don't be so impulsive. I didn't mean that literally. Sit down, sit down. Please." With his arm around my shoulders, he guided me back to my chair. The squeaky wheel gets the grease. "Tell me the whole story. Don't spare me the ghastly details."

"Did you know that David Turley audited Janus House four years ago?"

"David? That would be '72. Why, yes, I believe you're right."

"You didn't tell me that the other day."

"Is it important? If it is, I apologize. I just didn't think of it. You were quite free to look at . . . you're still free to look at David's complete employee file. That would show you everything he's ever worked on here."

"I don't think it will be necessary. The point I'm trying to make is that he's known Marianne Sprague since that time."

"Is that supposed to mean something?"

"Maybe. Maybe not. How well do you know Marianne Sprague?"

He turned as red as a thermometer plunged into hot water. "What do you mean how well? She's an old friend. I've known her at least ten years."

"Well, there's a nasty story going around that she's a nymphomaniac. That she beds down your auditors when they arrive to do the books. Right there on the premises of Janus House. That she enjoyed a special relationship with David Turley. That . . ."

"Stop!" Post was holding his hand up like a cop stopping traffic. He walked back behind his desk, sat in his chair, put his elbows on the desk, and bending his head, rested his forehead in his open palms. After a minute or two he raised his head. "I did know Marianne was a passionate woman and a bit eccentric. I knew she had many affairs. Look, Mr. Fletcher, she works hard. She's completely devoted to Janus House. She puts in sixty to eighty hours a week there. She doesn't have a family. She doesn't have much time to herself. When she plays, she plays hard. Do you blame her for that?"

"I don't judge her at all. I just want to know if her relationship to my client's brother is in any way connected to his death."

"What do you want me to do?"

"I'll get to that. There's more. Do you have any reason to suspect that Marianne Sprague is hooked?"

"God no! Hooked? On what?"

"Speed perhaps."

"Good God! Speed? No! I never heard of such a thing."

"How old is she?"

"Oh, she's young. Thirty-eight to forty."

"Yesterday you told me her energy was preternatural. Speed could explain that."

"I know absolutely nothing about such matters," he snapped.

"How about the relationship between Sprague and Robie Jeanette?"

"That's easy. They hated each other."

"Wasn't it intolerable for them to have to share Janus House all these years? Why did the board allow it?"

"It was expedient. The board believes in the Janus House program, Mr. Fletcher. Mr. Jeanette was in a position to embarrass us in the media. That would hurt the program. The uneasy truce we worked out was by far a preferable solution to our problem than severing Jeanette's ties with Janus House. After all, they did share different lines of authority. And the treatment aspects of the program are in Marianne's hands."

"Do you know what Jeanette earned?"

He closed his eyes as if in pain. "All too well."

"Do you know how much work he did?"

"All too well," he repeated.

"Isn't this nothing but blackmail?"

122

"Your characterization, Mr. Fletcher, not mine. I prefer to call it coming to grips with the political realities of twentieth-century America."

"Bullshit," I said.

"What!" he gasped.

"Bullshit," I repeated. I was trying to get him confused, upset, disoriented. I wanted to see what would happen when I put him on the defensive. "Guys like you just don't know how to deal with guys like Jeanette. All he had to do was act a little aggressive and shout a little and you caved in. You gave him whatever he wanted."

"Mr. Fletcher, this country has a long history of suppression of its minorities. No one has suffered from the results of this suppression more than the blacks. It doesn't hurt to make gestures to redress . . ."

"Bullshit!" I repeated it more loudly this time.

"Really, Mr. Fletcher, if you think your use of such gutter language . . ."

"Look, Jeanette was a racketeer, pure and simple."

"How can you say that? The man's record was clean. Why he never even had a parking ticket."

"That doesn't surprise me. He knew how to put the fix in. It doesn't surprise me that you didn't know how to deal with him either. Your kind never does. You have to hire people to do that."

"Really, Mr. Fletcher, Mr. Jeanette was a respected member of the black community. A bit flamboyant, perhaps, but . . ."

"Bullshit."

"Must you persist in using . . ."

"He controlled every government dollar that came into Gamintown. He had a lock on the school board there. He dispensed patronage through his club."

"All perfectly legitimate activities."

"Bullshit!"

123

"Mr. Fletcher, I must insist . . ."

"He was a racketeer, but you don't want to deal with that. You chose to coopt him by giving him certain tokens of esteem and prestige. In return he kept the Gamintown blacks off your block."

"Don't be absurd, I live in . . ."

"Greenwich? Saugatuck? Don't be so literal. You know what I mean."

"I most certainly do not."

"Well, let me spell it out for you. Jeanette had his hands on the levers of power in Gamintown. He was dynamic, aggressive, tough, smart—a natural leader. It wasn't too long ago that he was leading banner-waving hordes to City Hall to sit in and make demands. That scared guys like you. A bunch of crazy blacks carrying clubs and samurai swords demanding their rights. Tearing up the offices, shitting in the wastepaper baskets, raising hell in general."

"I can assure you, we've never had anything like that here at Post-McBride."

"And you never will as long as you have guys like Jeanette acting as a buffer for you. He can turn demonstrations on and off as easily as you can turn your water taps on and off."

"In addition to behaving boorishly, you're being just plain silly," said Post. He puffed furiously on his pipe. "How can one man control the activities of these hordes of blacks you say are ready to . . . to what, Mr. Fletcher?"

"Get a bigger slice of the pie," I said.

"What you're saying is that Jeanette got a bigger slice of the pie for himself because he helped . . . I suppose 'us' is the right word . . . helped us to prevent the other blacks from getting a bigger slice for themselves."

"That's right."

"I appeal to your reason, Mr. Fletcher. How can one man control so many people? People who you probably think are getting screwed?"

"You know how it works as well as I do. He controlled the jobs in Gamintown. He had his cadre of supporters on the payroll of the school boards, the community corporations, and the rest. What he wanted he got. If they didn't cooperate with him they were fired. If they did cooperate they kept their jobs. The rest of the people in Gamintown have no leader. They're not united. They fight among themselves to be first on line at the welfare center."

"You have a rather inflamed world view," he said calmly.

It wasn't working. He wasn't disturbed at all. At least not about what was happening in Gamintown and places like it. He didn't like the situation at Janus House. *That* affected him personally. Gamintown didn't. No. I gave him one parting shot before I changed my tactics. "You really don't want to redress grievances. You want people like Jeanette to keep things going the way they always have." I raised my voice to a near shout. "Now, what's the story between you and Marianne Sprague?"

He certainly wasn't expecting it. His pipe fell from his hand and the live ashes burnt a hole in the blotter of his desk set. "Please, Mr. Fletcher," he said, shushing me with his hand. "Don't talk like that. People might misunderstand. They can hear you out there." He pointed to the closed door of his office. He meant the anteroom where his secretary and a small staff of underlings sat.

"It didn't surprise you when I said Marianne Sprague was a nympho!" I yelled. "You knew it because . . ."

His face was pale, and his eyes were looking frantically at the door as though the weight of thousands of eavesdroppers with their ears pressed to it would burst it open. "Hush! Hush! I beg of you. Lower your voice!" He spoke in a high-pitched whisper. "What do you want to know?"

"I want to know about you and Marianne Sprague," I said in a normal conversational tone.

"All right," he said. He cleared his throat and tittered nervously. "All right." He used the speaking voice he had been using earlier. "As you suspected, we had an affair."

"How long ago was that?"

"It was a good ten years ago."

"How long did it last?"

"Not long. Not long at all. She was rather . . ." He cleared his throat again. "Shall we say demanding?"

"Insatiable?" I asked.

"That's probably a more apt description. And even ten years ago I had reached the age where amiability was more important than the kind of intensity and passion that Marianne offered."

"She's not a friend of your wife's then?"

"She is now. She wasn't then."

"After she started Janus House she sought you out. You and others like you, prominent and respected citizens, to serve on the board of Janus House?"

"Yes, that's the way it happened."

"Then she's using you, isn't she?"

"Well, not exactly. But, yes, to a certain extent, I suppose that's true."

"Do you really care about Janus House, its members, its program?"

"Why yes, of course I do."

"As a member of the board your own personal reputation and that of Post-McBride is tied to that of Janus House, isn't it?"

126

He held his head in the palms of his hands again. "Please don't remind me," he groaned.

"This news about Jeanette, about the fraud. How is it going to go down?"

"What?" He looked up at me.

"How will the board handle it? How will it affect you? What will it mean to Post-McBride?"

He had almost completely regained his composure. "The board will handle it with quiet dignity. Marianne will be returned to her original title of director. It's just unfortunate that we were betrayed by someone in whom we placed our trust, someone who, after all, we were only trying to . . . to . . ."

"Give a break to?"

"Those aren't the words I'd use, but they are apt. We were trying to give him a position of responsible leadership that would enable him to . . ."

"To what?"

"To be an example to his people," he concluded lamely.

Some example! "Go on," I said.

"Go on with what?"

"What effect will all this have on you?"

"On me? On me personally? Very little, I should imagine. It's distressing of course, but . . ."

"I think you're forgetting something."

"What's that?"

"This is a big story. It's going to attract a lot of attention. Reporters will be asking a lot of questions. Lots of heat will be put on the cops to tie things up."

"So?"

"So that will stir things up. It didn't take me long to find out about Sprague's sexual proclivities. It won't take others long either. It didn't take me long to find out she's a dope fiend."

"Please! Don't say that! Dope fiend. I swear I never heard anything about . . ."

"How do you think it's going to look? The president of Post-McBride on the board of a completely discredited operation. And God only knows what else is going to surface. You might know that better than I." It wasn't true of course. If the cops could nail Jeanette as Turley's murderer, Jeanette's suicide would cap the story sensationally, but that would be the end of it. It wouldn't be a continuing story. If Jeanette had lived things would have been different. The story would have dragged on for months.

"What are you driving at, Mr. Fletcher?" He spoke in a hard voice, using his best chief executive tones.

"Consider this scenario: none of the auditors knew what Jeanette was doing. You've always taken a personal interest in Janus House. Why, you even looked at this year's audit before Avildsen saw it. I'm sure that's not Post-McBride SOP."

"No, but . . ."

"Over the years, putting together bits and pieces of information contained in different audit reports, you became suspicious of billings from three organizations. You investigated further and found that these outfits were owned by Jeanette's relatives. You then pinned the butterfly and discovered the phantom billings. I did it, and I'm no accountant. You stewed for a long time, and finally decided to do something about it. You put that list with the names of the three businesses on Turley's bureau drawer to make it look as though he knew about the whole thing. You then lured him out to Gamintown on some pretext and shot him, knowing that the list would be discovered and its contents deciphered. The most obvious explanation for Turley's death, then, is that Turley attempted to blackmail Jeanette, Jeanette balked, and killed him so that he wouldn't talk."

"Mr. Fletcher, you just went to great lengths to explain to me the embarrassment I will face when it becomes common knowledge that Jeanette was defrauding Janus House and that Post-McBride failed to pick it up. Why would I do something that would bring the whole thing to light?"

"First, Jeanette was becoming more and more of an irritant to you. Second, you sat on the information you had too long and were scared by that grand jury that's been convened to look into Jeanette's activities. If the grand jury turned up evidence of Jeanette's fraud, the D.A. might start asking a lot of questions. It might draw the same conclusions as I have: that you've known about the fraud for some time. That story would be even more embarrassing than the disclosure that you were duped by Jeanette."

"Mr. Fletcher, that doesn't sound to me like a good enough motive for murder."

"There's more. Your primary motive was jealousy."

"Jealousy? Mr. Fletcher, I fear for your sanity. Of whom was I jealous?"

"David Turley. Look, you've told me that you severed your connection, your amoral connection, with Marianne Sprague ten years ago, but I don't believe it." It wasn't a shot in the dark. It was a hunch. It was the best play I had. So I made it.

He spoke slowly, carefully, underlining each word, *"You. Don't. Believe. It?"*

"No. There's an easy way, there's a hard way. Do you want me to dig around until I've proven it? It won't be hard to do, but in doing it more people might learn about it than you would like. That's the hard way. The easy way is for you to cooperate with me. If you do, and you're not the murderer, I might find the real murderer, and quickly. That's to your advantage. The quicker it's wrapped up, the less publicity it . . ."

His panic-stricken eyes roamed around the office, looking everywhere but at me. "You're despicable!" he said, standing up to his full height and finally looking me in the eye.

"You want it the hard way, then?" I gave him my best tough guy stare.

He held my gaze for a moment, then weakened, closing his eyes and holding his hand to his head before collapsing back in the chair. Sometimes the stare *still* works. "All right, Mr. Fletcher, you win. Yes, I still see Marianne occasionally."

"And you were jealous of Turley, weren't you? Jealous that he was the favorite among Sprague's lovers?"

"Yes, I was jealous," he gasped. "But that doesn't mean that . . ."

He couldn't finish his statement, but I knew he would cooperate.

Chapter 19

O'GARRITY was nervous. He wasn't used to being this close to the head man. His face was in a state of imminent collapse: the flesh under his chin sagged; his bloodhound eyes drooped; his lips formed a thin downward arc. And yet he was no more than thirty. "You asked to see me, Mr. Post?" he asked shyly. His small round eyes were the color of dark cough drops. They looked very unhappy.

"Yes, Marty, I'd like you to answer a few questions for Mr. Fletcher. He's a private investigator who's been hired by the family to look into the death of Dave Turley. You've heard about it, I take it?"

"Oh, yes sir. Quite a tragedy. Whatever you say, sir."

I wondered if all accountants kissed ass like that, or whether his obsequious behavior was peculiar to Post-McBride, or whether it was just an expression of O'Garrity's own personality.

"Now some of Mr. Fletcher's questions will be a little personal," said Post, "but I'd be *most* appreciative if you would cooperate with him."

"Oh, yes sir, if you say so." O'Garrity's voice had a

dying fall so that his sentences ended in a low mutter that required my full concentration to decipher.

"Go ahead, Mr. Fletcher," said Post.

"Mr. O'Garrity, you did an audit of Janus House two years ago, didn't you?"

"Yes, Mr. Fletcher. It was in 1974, about this time of year."

"Was there anything unusual about the audit?"

"No sir."

"You met Mr. Jeanette, didn't you?"

"Yes sir."

"What did you think of him?"

"Think of him? What do you mean?"

"Did he do his job well?"

"I'm not exactly sure what his job was."

"How often did you see him?"

"As I recall, he came in once a week in the mornings. I didn't see much of him."

"Was he friendly?"

"Oh, yes sir, quite friendly and open."

"How about Miss Sprague? Did you see much of her?"

He looked at me suspiciously and glanced sideways toward Post before answering. "As I recall she came in every day," he said.

"Did you talk to her much?"

"Often enough."

"What kind of a person was she?"

"Oh, she was very bright and articulate."

"Was she warm, friendly, outgoing?"

O'Garrity looked at a spot on the carpet a few inches from his shuffling feet. "Yes," he mumbled.

"What!" I said.

"She was friendly," he said.

"How friendly?"

"I don't know what you mean."

"Was she very friendly?"

"Yes," he said, shuffling his feet some more. His eyes were still riveted on the carpet.

"Was she more than friendly?"

He coughed, rubbed his palms on his thighs, and mumbled something unintelligible.

"What?" I asked.

He raised his eyes from the floor and looked at a spot somewhere between myself and Post. "Do I really have to answer these questions, sir?" he asked.

"No, you don't, Marty," said Post sympathetically. "Mr. Fletcher is not trying to embarrass you though, and I certainly appreciate *personally* any help you could give Mr. Fletcher in finding David Turley's killer."

O'Garrity's eyes went back to the spot on the rug. "Go ahead, Mr. Fletcher," he said. "What do you want to know?"

"Were you ever intimate with Marianne Sprague?"

He nodded his head affirmatively.

"More than once?"

He nodded again, but still said nothing.

"How often?"

"A lot," he mumbled.

"Can you tell me how it came about?"

"Well, it was after I was there about three days. I was working late. It was about six o'clock." His voice was low and his words came out of his mouth faster than bullets come out of a grease gun. "We were the only ones there on that floor. The area is off limits to everyone else at Janus House unless you're told to come. She asked me some questions about setting up a business. We talked maybe ten minutes. Then she suggested we have a drink. I said O.K." He turned to Post. "I had finished all I had planned for that day, Mr. Post."

"I'm sure you did. Go on, son," said Post smoothly.

"We went into Jeanette's office, and the next thing I knew . . . I don't know how it happened. . . . We were on a couch . . . uh." He stopped.

"Would it be fair to say she seduced you?" I asked. He nodded.

"Have you maintained your relationship with her?"

"I haven't seen her since 1974."

"Who was responsible for breaking off the relationship?"

"It was mutual. It was her idea, but I couldn't argue with it. She was very . . . uh . . . intense, Mr. Fletcher. Quite frankly, I don't have the energy for a woman like that. Besides, I didn't like her much," O'Garrity looked toward Post, but could get no reading on him. Post was leaning back in his chair, hands clasped behind his head, neck bent backward, face pointing toward the ceiling. His eyes were closed.

"You didn't like her? What didn't you like about her?"

"She was kind of cold-blooded, and tough, and bossy."

"Cold-blooded? From your description of your tussle on the couch, cold-blooded doesn't sound like an accurate . . ."

"Oh, no, I'm not talking about sex. I mean the way she treated people."

"What people? You mean the members?"

"Well, yes, the members too."

"Example?"

"She seems to specialize in breaking the spirit of the members. She expects absolute obedience to her dictates. If she doesn't receive it, she really cracks down. She loves to humiliate and degrade them."

"How do you know? After all, you spent your time

on the top floor of the mother house. You couldn't have seen her in action with the members."

"It was her attitude toward them. Very callous. And the stories she told me."

"What kind of stories?"

He was silent for a moment, frowning in thought. "I've tried to forget as much about that woman as I can. She really demeans you. Things she says." His voice trailed off. "Things she does. She's cruel. Quite frankly, she's a bitch."

Post changed his position, leaning forward once again with his elbows on the desk. He sighed heavily.

O'Garrity looked at him apprehensively. "I'm sorry, Mr. Post," he said. "It's just that . . ."

"Don't be silly, Marty. There's no need for you to apologize. I understand. I really do. I sympathize with you. We all know women like that. . . . I mean know that such women exist. Don't we, Fletcher?"

I ignored his question. "You were going to tell us about the stories she told."

"Yes, I remember one now. About how she handled one of her member-therapists she thought had been disloyal."

"What had he done?" I asked.

"Do you know it was so insignificant I can't remember? But the punishment I remember."

"What was it?"

"She made him shave off all his hair."

"Shave off all the hair on his body?"

"No, just on his head, but there was more. She made him wear a sign for a month that said, I don't know, 'I am a liar' or something like that. And she made him stand on his head."

"Stand on his head?"

"Yes, down by the switchboard where you come in. For a whole month during his lunch hour he had to

135

stand on his head. She really loved making him do that." O'Garrity shuddered.

"Did you and Miss Sprague ever have relations any place but in Jeanette's office?"

"No. Only there. It was spooky. She seemed to get some kind of kinky thrill out of it. You just had to walk in there with her and she was, uh, ready."

Friedman was a tall, bony young man, handsome in a rugged way, with a pair of alert brown eyes and an unruly mop of curly black hair.

After Post gave him the pitch, Friedman turned to me and said with a grin, "Fire away, Mr. Fletcher."

Friedman said he had done the Janus House audit in 1975. He had found nothing unusual. He had seen Jeanette once a week, on Monday mornings.

"How about Marianne Sprague?" I asked. "Did you see much of her?"

He hesitated a moment before he said, "Yes, I saw her every day."

"Was she friendly?"

"Very friendly."

"Was she more than friendly?"

"I think it would be fair to describe her that way."

"Look, Mr. Friedman," I said, "you know I'm trying to find David Turley's murderer. In order to do so, I'm learning as much as I can about Janus House, Marianne Sprague, and Robie Jeanette. We've been told that Miss Sprague systematically beds down the auditors sent in by Post-McBride to do the annual Janus House audit. She used Jeanette's office for this purpose. Can you confirm or deny this story?" I was getting impatient. I didn't like pulling teeth as I had with O'Garrity. Besides, I figured Friedman would be susceptible to the direct approach.

"Yes, Mr. Fletcher, the story is true. At least it's

true as far as I'm concerned. There's no question in my mind but that the woman is a nymphomaniac."

"Why do you say that?"

"The urgency of her need without regard to time or place. She wasn't interested in preliminaries. She wanted action—now! As soon as I was ready, she was ready. And as soon as we were finished, she was ready again. She told me once, and she was only half kidding, that the perfect lover for her would be a sixteen-year-old sex maniac."

"This always happened on the premises of Janus House? In Jeanette's office?"

"Always. At least with me."

"Where in Jeanette's office?"

"Anywhere. The floor. A couch, a chair. It didn't matter."

"Did she talk to you much?"

"She didn't really have a lot to say."

"Have you seen her since you did the audit?"

"Oh, no."

"Why not?"

"She's not really very pleasant, Mr. Fletcher. She has a tongue like sandpaper. She attacks: your performance, the way you look, anything."

I was finished with Friedman. I didn't know if I was finished with Post.

I left.

Chapter 20

Across the street from Post-McBride was a restaurant with bagel-shaped windows—one of a chain of "Mr. Bagel" emporiums. I like lox. I like cream cheese. I like bagels. I had never eaten in one of the new bagel restaurants that were cropping up all over town, but I hadn't eaten since the day before and was in a hurry, so I decided to give it a try.

It was outlandishly overdecorated with a heterogeneous mixture of natural wood paneling, mirrors, a flood of bright yellow lighting simulating sunshine, and a mixed bag of cheap antiques. Suspended from the ceiling in jute or macrame slings were a variety of lush green plants. The bushy-tailed tassels of the slings hung as low as my face and forced me to trace a zigzag route to the sloppy self-service cafeteria counter.

The skimpy slices of lox were dry and cracked and streaked with gray. I decided to pass the lox and ordered a bagel with cream cheese and tea. The bagel was huge and puffy, and tasted more like white bread than a bagel. The cream cheese was watery and tasteless. Even the tea was lousy.

I knew better. I knew that mass production and

mass distribution techniques invariably resulted in food scarcely fit for human consumption, but I was occasionally suckered into one of the plastic dens that specialized in such fare. For the umpteenth time I vowed to avoid such traps in the future. I realize that few can even occasionally aspire to the gustatory delights offered by Marshall Fong's Cantonese supreme, but that's no reason why I should debase my taste and insult my stomach by submitting them to the ersatz provender offered by Mr. Bagel.

Simultaneously swallowing my disappointment and dyspepsia I hopped into a cab and got off uptown at the main Janus House.

The woman on the switchboard was the same one who had been there the day before. The one Lambert had identified as Florence.

"Hello, Florence. It is Florence, isn't it? How are you?"

"How did you know my name?" she asked.

"I spoke to Garth Lambert today," I said.

"Oh, him!" she snorted contemptuously. "What's he doing these days?"

"Why don't we talk about it later when I'm through with Miss Sprague?"

"I haven't had dinner yet. I get off at five."

"I should be through with Miss Sprague by then. Suppose I take you to dinner?"

Marianne Sprague was waiting for me at the top of the stairs. Her secretary, Mrs. Dowd was busy at the typewriter.

"Well, Mr. Fletcher, how nice to see you again so soon. Wally Post told me you might be dropping by. What can I do for you?" She was smiling coquettishly.

"Just spare me a few more minutes of your time, if you will."

"More questions, Mr. Fletcher?"

"I'm afraid so."

"Don't you get tired spending your days as an information-gathering device?"

"Not at all. That's what being a detective is all about. Ask questions, get answers."

"Surely there's more to it than that?"

"The questions have to be the right ones. You have to evaluate the answers. You have to ask the questions suggested by the answers. You have to know when people are lying, when they are telling the truth. When they've really forgotten something, and when they only say they've forgotten. When they're being evasive, when they're distorting, and in what direction.

"Why, Mr. Fletcher, that sounds almost like what I do as a therapist. Come with me, you interesting man, and ask me your questions." She clutched my upper arm with both hands and, leaning her weight on my arm, led me to her office.

"I'm not to be disturbed, Harriet," she said over her shoulder to Mrs. Dowd, "until Mr. Fletcher is through with me. Or vice versa," she added.

She still wore heavy jewelry that clanked and jangled at every step, but yesterday's peasant costume had been replaced by a one-piece black body stocking. A crinkly lime green chiffon skirt bouffant-styled, covered the area from her hips to her knees. A bright yellow sailcloth vest attempted to cover her breasts, but whenever she made a sudden movement, they were revealed in all their braless glory as hard and as firm as two unripe melons. In fact, her whole body was as trim and taut as a teenager's, a tribute to her genes, her exercise program, her diet, or all three. It wasn't hard to see why the young accountants from

Post-McBride had not made heroic efforts to reject her advances.

She led me to the couch in front of the window, sat down, and patted it to indicate where she wanted me to sit. I had no choice. The only other places to sit were at her desk or in one of the chairs arranged around her desk.

"I think we'll be able to chat more comfortably here, don't you, Mr. Fletcher?"

Her hoyden's face was kissing close, and the scent from her body gave me ideas that had nothing to do with finding David Turley's murderer. I edged away from her slightly. No good. She followed me. A crazy light danced in back of her eyes. Her lips stretched into a smile that revealed her sharp little teeth. She was really enjoying it.

"You're not going to run away, are you Mr. Fletcher?"

That was exactly what I thought about doing, but a headlong retreat to the area of her desk would not be too dignified. "No, but you are a bit too close for comfort." I edged a little further away.

She followed. "I'll make a deal with you, Mr. Fletcher," she said, grabbing my right hand in both of hers. "You call me Marianne, I'll call you Virgil, and I'll give you a little breathing space." Her eyes were dancing with pleasure and amusement.

"Agreed," I said.

"This should be a very pleasant experience. Unusual, but pleasant." She stretched her upper body, as lithe as a cat, neck arched backward, back bowed, arms raised to shoulder height, elbows then bent, shoulders pushed until elbows touched. She held that pose for a moment before she let it go, raising her arms overhead and flexing her fingers, before, true to her word, she edged a bit away from me.

"If you're trying to raise my pulse, you've succeeded," I said. "In fact it didn't require all that effort."

"Oh, don't be silly, Virgil, that's just my stretching routine. It recharges my batteries."

"They need recharging?"

"Virgil, I'm forty-three. I've led a full life already. I've worked very hard. I've had professional recognition. I've written three books. I enjoy a certain degree of fame. But do you know I'm almost as proud of the fact that I've kept my body this way as I am of those other things?"

I looked at her face. Hard. Her face looked its age, maybe older. Wasted by fatigue and hard work. And more? The uppers that Lambert talked about? "That's understandable," I said.

"You certainly don't throw around compliments, do you?"

It was no good. She was in control. I was supposed to be in control. If I wasn't in control I wasn't doing my job. "The detective should always be in control." You could look it up. That's what it says in *The Detective Manual*. O.K. One good way to take control was to blast her. I did. "Why didn't you tell me that you and David Turley were lovers?" I asked.

Her pale eyes widened, then narrowed. She gazed at me appraisingly, almost imperceptibly shaking her head up and down as she did so. "You really are a detective, aren't you?"

I said nothing.

"Virgil, why on earth do you think I should have told you that?"

"It's true, isn't it?"

"That's beside the point. Why should I have told you? As I recall, you never even asked me."

Cute. She was very cute. Years of practicing therapy had made her adept at all kinds of verbal games. What else could you expect? She wasn't just a shrink, she had a law degree too. I would have to keep things simple. *Very* simple.

"When I talked to you yesterday you made believe you didn't even know his name. You called him Tully."

"Was that naughty of me, Virgil? Virgil?" she suddenly asked. "Virgil?" She held the name at arm's length and examined it with disgust. "Virgil!" She dropped it with a crash. "What the hell kind of a name is that? You sound like some hayseed who belongs on a farm in . . ."

"Bumfuck?" I interrupted.

"What?" she said.

"Bumfuck," I repeated.

"Bumfuck?"

"Idaho. Bumfuck, Idaho. Virgil is a name that belongs to a buy who comes from Bumfuck, Idaho."

A rich deep sound forced its way up from somewhere inside her. She didn't want it to come. She tried holding it back by placing both hands over her mouth, but it leaked between her fingers and mixed with the barking snuffs that came through her nostrils. Finally, she could contain it no longer and fell against the couch, elbows and neck resting on the top of the back, head lolling, legs widespread. Peal after peal of ringing laughter bounced off the walls. Her pale face reddened, and freshets of tears sprang from her eyes and rolled down her cheeks. Unable to control herself, she sprang from the couch and forced herself to take deep shuddering hiccuppy breaths. With one final deep sigh she brought her laughter under control and flung herself back down on the couch next to me.

"Virgil," she said, "You ain't gonna be easy! Bumfuck? Idaho? Bumfuck! Idaho! That's priceless!"

"You called him Tully," I said.

"What was I supposed to do, Virgil? Start confessing my sins to you like some character from a Dostoevsky novel? Not on your horse collar I wasn't."

"Not on my sump pump."

"What?"

"Sump pump. Sump pumps are very big with the modern farmer. Horse collars are out. Have been for years. No, you didn't have to do that. But what you did do was foolish. It looks suspicious."

"Why should it look suspicious? You were looking for a missing man. I had no idea where David was, but I was sure he would turn up. I had no information to help you. It would have been indiscreet of me to tell you about David and me. I never thought this kind of a scandal would develop."

"You don't seem to be too upset by David Turley's death."

"Upset? Oh, I'm a little upset. What do you expect me to do, wear widow's weeds? We were simply willing and eager bedmates, Virgil. There was little emotional attachment on either of our parts. I'm sorry David's dead. It leaves a void in my life. But life goes on. My work goes on."

"Did David Turley ever tell you that Jeanette was bilking Janus House by using its funds to pay phony invoices?"

"No, but Wally Post just called and told me."

"Do you have any reason to believe that David Turley was blackmailing Jeanette?"

"No."

"A list was taped to the bottom drawer of the dresser in Turley's bedroom. The list was identified by the initials 'J.H.' and 'R.J.' Janus House and Robie Jeanette. There were three names on the list. They were the names of the organizations sending the

144

phony bills to Jeanette. Do you know anything about that?"

"Only what you're telling me, and what Wally Post told me."

"The police suspect that Robie Jeanette killed Turley because Turley was blackmailing him."

"So I've heard."

"What do you think of that theory?"

"If they suspect him, they must have some reason for it."

"Do you think Jeanette was capable of murder?"

"I most certainly do! There's no question in my mind about that."

"Why?"

"I'd known him for years. He was egotistical, irresponsible, temperamental, unscrupulous, and totally untrustworthy."

"And he had halitosis."

"What?"

"Never mind. Why did you hate him so?"

"Why? I've just told you."

"You weren't very specific."

"Look, Virgil, it's no secret that Robie and I had no use for each other. I never liked him. He never liked me. Janus House is mine, Virgil!" She was speaking in a hoarse passionate whisper. "Mine, do you hear! My ideas, my passions, my talents, my strength, my blood built Janus House. And Jeanette was a parasite who fed on my beautiful creation."

"But surely he must have served some useful purpose? Like in this new Gamintown Janus House?"

"Yes. He was good at finding new houses."

"How did he go about it?"

"He dealt only with slumlords. He threatened and squeezed them."

"How?"

145

"Oh, he had a variety of methods. Most of them involved threats of demonstrations directed against the landlords or leaking stories about their activities to the media."

A very effective technique. Some slumlord who lives out in Great Neck does not want a couple of busloads of welfare clients, Janus House members, and employees of Jeanette's various community organizations marching on his front lawn trampling the tulip beds, waving picket signs, and chanting slogans. He wants even less to be identified by the media as an entrepreneur who reaps tidy profits by providing squalid housing at excessive rent to the people at the bottom of the heap. As long as Jeanette hadn't been too outrageous in his demands he probably got wise slumlords to make a number of significant concessions, when the alternative was a distinctly unpleasant experience whose repercussions were unfathomable. Like shylocks, slumlords prefer to work in anonymity, away from the glare of publicity.

"He wanted the Gamintown house to be his greatest coup," she continued. "He didn't want anyone to see it until it was actually ready to take in members. You can bet he planned to make a big fuss about it," she added bitterly. "Newspaper coverage, TV, celebrity ribbon cutting, the works. He even tried to make it the mother house, and interfered with my therapy by having individual telephones installed all over the place. Forgetting the expense, that's poor therapy. Addicts need discipline, not that kind of coddling. A switchboard is a very valuable therapeutic tool. It teaches the addicts to respect each other's privacy. It's so important that the job of switchboard operator is one of the most prestigious positions a member can hold at Janus House—we have to be sure that the person on the switchboard is reliable and won't listen in on other members' conversations. It makes me furious. He'd never been successful before this in his attempts to interfere with my therapeutic techniques."

"Why was he this time?"

"Because the board decided the question of telephones fell into his bailiwick, that it had nothing to do with therapy. But it does. It does. It's obvious. Why even his arguments were based on my ideas of how to increase the dignity and self-respect of the members. Absurd! *No one* knows how best to do that but me!"

Her *chutzpa* was boundless. No one could ever know how to do anything better than she did. "Why did you put up with Jeanette for so many years?"

" 'Put up with' is too passive a description of my attitude toward sharing the Janus House directorship with Jeanette. He was rammed down my throat by the board year after year when it was contract renewal time."

"Well, why did you let that happen? Surely, with your fame, your reputation, with the respect you enjoy, you could have pulled out of Janus House anytime and started all over again."

"But if I had done that, Janus House would have died. Can a mother slay her own beloved child?"

"Why did you let a board get involved in the first place?"

"It happened in the early days. I was desperate for funds. The most expedient way to get the money that I needed for Janus House was to get distinguished, rich, famous people to help Janus House. There was a *quid pro quo*. You don't get something for nothing. I got the names I needed, the help I needed, but I had to make concessions."

"Jeanette was one of those concessions?"

"Certainly not! I would never have agreed to him.

147

No, the primary concession I made was to allow the board the power to name 'the major officers of Janus House.' That's how our charter reads. I didn't even think about it. After all, I *was* Janus House before the board even existed. I had a clause inserted in the charter which puts me, by name, in charge of all ongoing therapeutic activities that take place at Janus House. Had I been prescient, had I known that Jeanette would appear on the doorstep . . ." Her voice trailed off.

"You hated him because you had to share the directorship, is that it?"

"I think I would have a problem dealing with anyone as a co-director of my organization. What right does *anyone* have to tell me how to run this place?" She was more than confident that she was right. She had an arrogant intellectuality that would not admit the possibility that she was wrong. "But *Jeanette*? He made positive efforts to undermine my authority, to have the members revolt against me. He tried to take over Janus House himself. My creation!"

"Then you're not surprised about the three partnerships Jeanette set up for his relatives? The phony bills these outfits submitted for payment by Janus House?"

"I'm not surprised at all. As I said, untrustworthy, a petty grafter and cheap hoodlum—that's all he ever was."

"Did you suspect that something like this was going on?"

"I didn't suspect. I didn't think about it. I think about the members, the terrible habit they've acquired, the contribution to society they can make if they're cured. I don't think about business matters."

"How was Jeanette able to handle his duties in a couple of hours a week?"

"He had nothing do do."

"I should think he had a lot to do. Just in terms of, say, ordering supplies, for instance."

"All he did was write checks. The members did everything else, including the payroll. They had to order from his list of approved vendors, of course!"

"That seems to bother you."

"It does. Last year our house in the Bronx had some problems with its boiler. It was the middle of winter, and it was freezing. It was a weekend. The members called Jeanette's vendor but got no answer. They called several times. Finally, they brought someone else in to do the job. Jeanette was furious. He refused to sign a check to pay the bill until the board made him."

"His suicide certainly works out nicely for you," I said. She was smarter than Post. She knew that outside of a few more big headlines the story was dead. No bird dogs would be camping on her doorstep digging into her private life.

"In what way?"

"The publicity? The scandal?"

"Virgil," she said. "The board hired a thief. The thief killed himself." Her eyes narrowed like a cat's, her lips stretched into a sly, gloating smile. I swear that I saw a few feathers drift to the floor from her lips. "We're all human, Virgil. We all make mistakes. Janus House made a mistake when it hired Jeanette. The public will forgive and forget."

"I'm talking about you. You and David Turley. You and Friedman. You and O'Garrity. The news will never come out now."

"I am thankful, Virgil, that for once in his life that man did the right thing." She hadn't turned a hair.

"What did you think about his suicide?"

"What about it?"

"He didn't seem to be the type."

"I don't know, Virgil. It would not be that unusual for a man like him to do away with himself under the stress of this kind of a situation."

"Come off it," I said. "What reason would he have?"

"I'm sick of talking about that man. I'm sick of this whole business."

"O.K., I'll change subjects. How did you feel about David Turley becoming his sister's manager and moving to the coast?"

"I must admit I was disappointed. But David had his own way to make in the world, just as I do." She shrugged. "He'll be hard to replace, maybe impossible. But I'll try, Virgil, I'll try."

"You didn't resent his leaving?"

"Of course not."

"In your liaisons with Friedman and O'Garrity you were the aggressor . . ."

"I'm *always* the aggressor, Virgil," she interrupted. "That's the way I like it."

"Yes. Well, it also seems that you were the one to cut them loose. Fast. Did it bother you that this time you were being dropped?"

"I don't think that 'dropped' properly describes what happened, Virgil."

"Is it fair to say that he initiated the break between you?"

"What he initiated was a change in his professional life that would mean that we would see less of each other, that's all."

"Didn't it bother you that he was the one to initiate the change?"

"Of course not. I admired him for it. I've always placed my professional life ahead of any personal considerations. So did David. Why should I resent him for doing what I would have done had I been in his place? Besides, it's not as though we would never see each other again. He'd be in New York on business from time to time. I occasionally have to go to the coast for conferences and the like."

"How often did you and David see each other?"

"At least once or twice a week. Sometimes more, never less."

"Did it bother you that you would now see much less of each other?"

"Oh yes, very much. It bothered David too. But, *c'est la vie.*"

"Was David aware of your activities with other men?"

"What do you know about my activities with other men?"

"Well, I know about Friedman and O'Garrity. What I know about them leads me to believe there must be others."

"Yes, there were others, and David knew it. As I said, we had a very special relationship. We talked about them. It was amusing, and flattering to David. None of them measured up to David, and I told him so."

"How about David? Was he active with other women?"

"To my knowledge, no. Oh, there were a few isolated instances here and there. But Virgil," she said with a dogmatic air, "I am more than enough woman for any man, even when the man is a performer like David Turley." She patted me on my arm. "You believe me, don't you, or should I prove it to you?"

"That won't be necessary."

"Oh, I know it's not ncessary, but it might be fun. All work and no play makes Virgil a dull boy." Her eyes were appraising me and mocking me at the same time. "Or are you afraid of being compared to others?

Compared by a woman who has a good basis for making comparisons?"

"I don't look at sex as some kind of performance contest between myself and the rest of the men in the world."

"That's unfortunate, Virgil. That's how I see it. A contest. There's no man that's completely unattractive to me. I like them all. They all have something to offer. I like to measure them against each other. There are very few that disappoint. Most of them are adequate. Some are stars. David, of course, was a phenom. Wouldn't you like to know how you rate?"

David was a phenom? So was she. I didn't know the numbers involved, but she sounded as though she were talking about armies. How did she have time for her nonsexual activities? I ignored her question. It was time to lead our conversation in another direction. "Can you tell me where you were last Friday afternoon and evening?"

"You just insist on sticking to business, don't you? That's all right, Virgil. I admire that. I *can* be patient, you know. You do whatever you think you have to do. It's silly. We all know who killed David. But do what you must. We'll see each other when you've finished that."

"How do you know?"

"Don't ask. I know."

There was that intellectual arrogance again. She knew everything. She thought she didn't have to consult anyone or anything. She could always stand alone, seeking no help and needing none. "Friday afternoon and evening?"

"Virgil, you're really being absurd, you know. Do you really think I'd destroy a stud like David? Never! He was too rare and special an individual."

"Where were you?"

"I have a perfect alibi Virgil. From early in the morning until ten at night I was at a one-day social work conference held by the United American Social Workers, the UASW."

"It seems unusual to hold a conference on the day before the July fourth weekend," I said.

"Not at all. Not this July fourth. Remember, it's the Bicentennial year," she replied. "Operation Sail. The fireworks display at the Battery."

"I get it. The organizations that employ the social workers pay their expenses to the junket, which just happens to allow them to be in the city for the Bicentennial festivities."

"Yes."

Why not? Why should social workers be any different from anyone else? There's nothing wrong with combining business with pleasure, is there? Or is there? How many would have attended if it had not been an extra-special weekend? On July fourth? Who would normally want to be in the city on the July fourth weekend? Not too many people. Not me. And who put up the money for this junket in the first place? You did. I did. Oh well, to each his own. "What happens at a conference?" I asked.

"You pay your fee, and then you have a choice of attending various seminars and lectures. In the evening the UASW had a dinner with a number of speakers. I conducted one of the seminars in the morning, I attended two lectures in the afternoon, and I was one of the speakers at the dinner. I was on the premises of Hudson Business College most of the day. I even brought a dress to wear at the dinner so I wouldn't have to go home and change."

"Why Hudson Business College?"

She shrugged. "I guess because it's conveniently located."

153

It is. Lower Manhattan. Near City Hall, the IRT, the BMT, and the tunnels and bridges leading to Jersey and the other boroughs. "Where was the dinner held?"

"In one of the banquet rooms of the Phoenix." She stood up. "Now, I hope you're done with your questions. As usual I'm behind schedule, and I'm already five minutes late for a group session."

"I don't want to hold you up. Thanks for your cooperation."

"Don't mention it."

Chapter 21

FLORENCE was waiting for me at the entrance. She was pouting. "You're twenty minutes late," she said.

"Sorry. Your boss talks a lot."

"Don't I know it."

"Any ideas for dinner?"

"How about Cat's Cradle?"

It was a soul food place a few blocks away on Broadway. I had never eaten there, but had heard good things about it. I was batting .000 in the food league that day, but Cat's Cradle promised something better than a total strike out. "Let's go," I said.

Before we got to Cat's Cradle, I stopped in a drugstore on Broadway, and called Janie Fulton at the UASW. It was after five, but Janie was a hard worker, and usually stayed late. I knew her from her days as a probation officer. She'd already been with UASW a few years and she owed me a favor.

"Virgil," she said when she got on the phone, "you naughty man. It's been years."

"Two," I said.

"What's up?"

"The UASW held a one-day conference last week,"

155

I said, "on July second. I wonder if you could tell me if a certain party attended it."

"That's easy to do. We have the names of everybody who was there. What's the name of your certain party?"

"Marianne Sprague."

"That's easy, Virgil. She was there all right. She gave a speech at our dinner that night. I even attended a seminar she conducted in the morning. 'Drugs, Crime, and the Urban Crisis.'"

"She says she was there all day."

"She probably was. Do you want me to check?"

"Can you tell me what she did in the afternoon?"

"I can check our records and find out," she said.

"Would you do that, Janie?" I asked.

"Sure. Anything else?"

Was I wrong, or was there a hopeful note in her voice? Probably not. We had been very tight at one time. We weren't right for each other. She knew it, and I knew it. "No. Thanks, anyway."

"Where will you be?"

"I don't know exactly. Can you call me at home later? If I'm not there, just leave a message with the answering service."

"At home? O.K., Virgil." Did she sound too eager? Once again, probably not. Just the professional social worker's standard tone of affable agreeability in fielding requests for assistance.

The lighting in Cat's Cradle was dim. The walls were paneled in dark wood. The tables were covered by red-checkered tablecloths. A candle in a glass container was on each table. Florence suggested family style. She had the chicken. I had the ribs. We split the greens, yams, potato salad, and rice. We both passed on the drinks. I didn't want alcohol in my empty stomach. I don't know what her reason was.

After we ordered, she said, "So how is old whey-face? He sounds as miserable as ever."

"You mean Garth Lambert?"

"Who do you think I mean, my Aunt Jemima?"

"Cut the crap," I said.

"All cops just love to talk tough and give orders. Cops and pimps. Only way to tell them apart is by the clothes they wear and the cars they drive."

I wanted to talk to her. I knew that she wanted to talk to me. I didn't know if she wanted to talk to me more than I wanted to talk to her, but I didn't think we'd get anywhere with this kind of dialogue. I stood up. "O.K., Florence, forget it." I stepped toward the door.

"Wait a minute!" she said, grabbing my sleeve. "Don't climb on your high horse. I'm sorry. Let's try again. How is Garth?"

"I don't know what he was like before, but I'd say he was unhappy, bitter, lonely, and worried."

"Some people just like to have the miseries."

"It's no fun being out of work, you know. He's afraid he'll wind up back in Jersey with his folks."

"My heart just bleeds for that man! College graduate. Accountant. Parents with some money. Mmmm-mm, that's sho' tough."

She wanted to talk about Lambert. I wanted to talk about other things. I figured she wouldn't talk about what I wanted to talk about until I talked about what she wanted to talk about. "Why don't you tell me about you and Garth Lambert?"

"Tell? There's nothing to tell. What's there for me to tell about that honky?"

"You think he let you down, don't you? Maybe he feels the same way about you."

"All I told him was the facts of life."

"What are they?"

157

She gave me a hard look but said nothing.

"How old are you, Florence?"

"Twenty-two."

"When did you go on the street?"

"Seven years ago. I was fifteen."

"When did you start shooting up?"

"My man. Not my first man, but my second. He had me snorting when I was sixteen. I was mainlining before I was seventeen."

"Any kids?"

"Two," she said tonelessly.

And probably a couple of abortions besides. "Do you know where they are?"

"No. I gave them away."

"When did you come to Janus House?"

"Three years ago."

"You've been off H all that time?"

"You better believe it."

Here was at least one success story for Marianne Sprague. "You must be very grateful to Marianne Sprague."

She coughed out a sharp, bitter laugh. "That cunt? Why?"

"Well, Janus House is her idea, her program."

"Let me tell you something, man. Janus House don't cure no addicts. We cure ourselves."

"If you weren't in Janus House do you think you'd be off drugs now?"

"No."

"Then Janus House helped you. Marianne Sprague helped you."

"Man, I paid for every bit of help I got."

"How?"

She glowered but said nothing.

"How come you're on the switchboard? I thought

158

the idea was for the members to work their way up the ladder as member-therapists?"

"The switchboard job is supposed to be a great honor," she said with a bitter laugh. "You know, you protect your fellow members' privacy, and all that jazz. What a crock!"

"Why is it a crock?"

"Well, if someone's not around to take a call we post any messages on the bulletin board."

I remembered the cork board on the wall to the right of the switchboard. It had contained a number of messages for the members and staff individually posted with thumbtacks. "What's wrong with that?"

"Well, the high and mighty Miss Sprague reads every one of them three times a day: when she comes in, when she goes out to lunch, and when she leaves."

"Do you think that violates the privacy principle?"

"Well, *her* messages don't go on the bulletin board."

She just didn't like Marianne Sprague. "O.K.," I said. "Maybe Sprague is nosy, but rank has its privileges and maybe it's one way for her to keep her fingers on the pulse of the Janus House community."

"Anyway," Florence continued, "I used to be a member-therapist. I'm on the switchboard as punishment."

"Punishment? You're on the . . . What did you do?"

"I complained."

"Complained? Complained about what?"

"The food."

"You didn't like the food?"

"I didn't like not having any."

"You weren't getting any food?"

"None of us were."

The waiter brought our food. "Look, Florence," I said, "it's going to be easier for both of us if you just

159

tell me what happened. Otherwise we can keep on Ohing and Ahing until midnight."

"O.K. A couple of months back she cut off all food at the mother house."

"She cut off all food! What do you mean? How could she do that?"

"By just saying no more food. She started on a Sunday. A starvathon she called it. No breakfast or lunch. Just supper. We always get cold cuts for Sunday supper. I don't dig cold cuts. It kept on like that. Missing lunches, breakfasts, suppers. Some days we got no food at all."

"What happened?"

"We encountered her."

"Who?"

"The members."

"And?"

"And she told us that we were just angry."

"Of course you were angry. So what?"

"She said that the anger was inappropriate. It showed we didn't trust her. That we were disloyal to Janus House."

Sure. And the Jews who were led to the gas ovens didn't trust their keepers, and were disloyal to Nazi Germany. Marianne Sprague was some case. "How did it all turn out?"

"Most of the members split. Those who didn't were thrown out."

"Thrown out. For what?"

"She said the members were taking it personal and attacking her personally. She threw them out."

"And you stayed?"

"I'm afraid of the street, man." Her eyes glistened with tears. "I don't want to go back. I had to accept or get thrown out. And she said I was strong."

"Why strong?"

"Because I accepted it. She said only the strong accepted the starvathon. The weak were thrown out for the good of the community."

My ribs were getting cold. So was her chicken. "And now you're being punished for protesting in the first place."

She nodded.

"Where is she getting member-therapists?"

"She brought them in from other houses."

"Is this why you hooked up with Lambert?"

"Uh-huh. Something like that. He could have been my ticket out. Besides . . ." She stopped.

"Besides what?"

"I've been at Janus House three years, man. You get lonely."

"No sex?"

She nodded.

A hyperactive nympho prohibits sex for the members while she systematically seduces the accountants from Post-McBride on the premises. Great! "What went wrong between you and Lambert?"

"It was too heavy for him, man. He couldn't take it."

"Your past?"

"Right. All he wanted was to ball me. Otherwise, he wasn't interested."

"And you wanted more?"

"A lot more."

"Maybe you laid it all on him too fast."

"Maybe."

"You'd like to try again?"

"Something like that."

"What do you see in the guy anyway? He's not exactly the answer to a maiden's prayer."

"I'm not a maiden, and I don't pray. I don't know, he seems a lot like me. A loser."

"You're not a loser, Florence. How many people break the drug habit?"

"Not many."

"Well, *you* have. That's winning, not losing."

"You're right, Mr. Fletcher. At least it's a victory. Sometimes I get on myself. You think I should forget about Garth?"

"You should do what you have to do. Personally, I think you're too good for him."

"I don't know why, but I feel a little better now that I've talked to you."

We were silent for a few minutes, concentrating on our food. "Did you ever hear of Freedom Maintenance?" I finally asked.

She looked at me quizzically. "I sure did," she said. "There was a big flap last winter. One of our houses in the Bronx had problems with the boiler. The members tried to get a hold of Freedom to fix it. They couldn't, so they called someone else. Jeanette blew his stack. We figured something was going on between him and Freedom."

"This is common knowledge at Janus House?"

"We get lots of changes at Janus House. People come and go. Members, staff, everybody. I've been there about as long as anybody. I knew about it because I was in the Bronx house at that time. I transferred down to the mother house as I worked my way up the ladder."

"So it's not common knowledge?"

"No. Some people know about it, but I don't know how many. Not many."

"Can you give me an estimate? Fifty? Twenty?"

"I'd say maybe ten or twelve. No more than that."

"No one knew the whole story? Knew that Freedom Maintenance was a partnership set up by Jeanette to bilk Janus House. That he set up other partnerships to do the same?"

"We figured something like that was going on. How come it wasn't on the TV?"

"The cops are sitting on it. They want to tie all this up into a neat little package before they give out all the facts."

"The cops *never* give out all the facts," she said dogmatically.

"Did anyone know, Florence?"

"I didn't know. I don't know if anyone knew. I don't think so."

"Why?"

"When you last there as long as I have, you have a pretty good idea of who knows what."

"Do you think Marianne Sprague knew about Freedom and the other outfits?"

"Sure."

"Why?"

"She knows everything else that goes on."

"Did you ever talk about Freedom to Garth Lambert?"

"In passing."

"What did he do about it?"

"He took it up with that other dude."

"Turley?"

"Yeah, that's the one."

"What happened then?"

"Turley told him to stop playing Dick Tracy. To mind his own business, and do his work."

"What did Lambert think of Turley's reaction?"

"He agreed with him. He chewed me out for bothering him with gossip. He said Turley didn't want to rock the boat, and neither did he. Garth was trying to score points with Turley. When Turley bit his head off, Garth bit mine off."

"Did Lambert give the impression that he thought Turley was covering something up?"

"Nothing like that. Turley just wanted him to get it on. Garth said that Turley thought he was just trying to stick around Janus House a few more days to goof off."

I took my last bite of the pecan pie. "How about Atlas Laundry and M&M Butchers? Ever hear of them?"

"Nope."

We finished our coffee. There didn't seem to be any place else to go. "Thanks, Florence, you've been a big help."

"How about helping me?" she asked.

"How?"

"You're going to see Garth again, aren't you?"

I sure was. I wanted to know why he hadn't told me about Freedom Maintenance, and his discussion about it with David Turley. I wanted to know if he had talked to anyone else about it. "Yes."

"Well, you can talk to him about me."

"I think it's better if you do that for yourself."

"He doesn't want to talk to me."

As far as I was concerned she was better off that way. "Look, forget it. What can I say?"

"I don't know," she said.

Neither did I. If I thought of something to say, I'd say it to Lambert. I didn't think of something, and I didn't want to raise false hopes in her. "Let's forget it then."

Her face stiffened. She stood up and flung her napkin to the table. "It's always a one-way street where you're concerned ain't it, whitey? All take, no give."

I said nothing.

She left.

Chapter 22

I WAS in the vestibule of Lambert's high-rise apartment building near Gramercy Park. He didn't answer my ring. I must have pushed the buttons of ten other apartments before the buzzer rang to let me in. When it did, I opened the door, tore a page from my notebook, folded it over eight times, and inserted it between the frame and the door itself. I took a walk around the block. When I returned, the folded paper still held the front door open. I put the paper into my pocket and entered the lobby. Somewhere in the back of my sensibility an acrid odor registered. It grew stronger as the elevator lifted me to Lambert's third floor apartment. The smell became a fine haze when the elevator door opened, and when I reached Lambert's door I found the source of the smell and the haze. Thin wisps of smoke curled from under the bottom of the door. It was steel and so was the frame. I shouldered it futilely a few times, then tried forcing it open by pounding it with some flat-footed kicks. Nothing happened. The TV detectives never have problems battering doors open.

The haze in the hall deepened and turned into light

smoke. There were seven other apartments on the floor. I yelled fire and banged on all the doors. A white-haired woman wearing a hearing aide opened the door to 3-A. She was dressed to go out. The smoke was beginning to make me cough. "Call 911," I hacked.

She slammed the door in my face. The name plate said: "O'Leary."

The occupants of several other apartments had already responded to my alarms and were crowding into the elevator I had just vacated. I was stuck with O'Leary.

I pressed the elevator button to get a car to stop on that floor and banged on her door again, pounding loudly until her round blue eye appeared in the peephole. "Go away," she said. "I don't want any." She closed the peephole.

"Lady," I yelled, pounding on the door more vigorously than before, "there's a fire in 3-E! Get out of here!" The smoke was getting thicker. I wrapped my handkerchief over my nose and mouth. As I did so the peephole opened again.

"Why are you wearing that mask?" said the woman behind the door.

"Fire!?" I yelled. "Fire!"

"Tire? I don't know anything about your tire."

"Smoke!" I yelled.

"I don't smoke," she said.

"The building's on fire, lady."

The peephole closed again. I raised my fist to pound on the door again, but before I could strike it the door opened, and she peered suspiciously around me. "Oh dear! Oh dear!" she exclaimed. She hadn't coughed yet. Maybe her imbecility conferred on her some kind of immunity to the effects of smoke inhalation.

I tried to hustle her to the elevator, but she

resisted, fumbling in her outsize shoulder bag. "Come on!" I said. I didn't want us to be found in the hall, overcome by smoke, when the firemen arrived.

"The keys!" she choked. Her apparent immunity to smoke had vanished. "The keys!" She finally pulled a key ring from the depths of her purse, and held them out to me. I took them from her, locked her door, and half carried her to the elevator. The door was open and a car waited for us.

As we descended to the lobby she muttered crankily about the rent she paid, and about the fact that the building had no doorman and no security so that "anyone could walk in." What bothered her most was "seeing two strangers on my floor in one day."

She glared at me and shuffled out of the building without a word. She didn't seem concerned about her apartment. I would have been. It takes all kinds.

I called Escalero from a bar that was on the ground floor of the building, and then talked to the residents of the other apartments on Lambert's floor. They were easy to pick out. They were huddled in a knot talking excitedly about the fire, strangers forced together by circumstances. Typical New Yorkers, none of them knew Lambert, except a few of them had nodded to him on the elevator from time to time. None had an inkling of how the fire had started.

The firemen arrived in a few minutes. It only took them ten minutes to put out the fire. A little later the meat wagon from the Medical Examiner's office came and drove off with a body bag that probably held what was left of Lambert.

Twenty minutes later Escalero arrived. He spotted me in the small crowd that had gathered across the street from the building, walked over to me and said, "This better be good, Virgil."

"I don't know if it's good," I said, "but it's something you should know about." The regulations called for an automatic autopsy whenever a suspicious or accidental death occurred. But it took time. Escalero could see to it that the autopsy was done immediately. I wasn't worried about getting a copy of the autopsy report itself. I had my own contacts to manage that.

"O.K., talk." He looked ten years older than he had the day before. His eyes were sunk in his head and were shadowed by dark rings of fatigue.

"The guy who did the Janus House audit for Post-McBride this year was named Garth Lambert. He lives in this building. Apartment 3-E. That apartment was just burnt out, and a body was just taken from it. I think it was Garth Lambert."

"So?"

"So, he had reason to believe that Jeanette was connected to Freedom Maintenance."

"Why?"

"This winter a boiler broke down in a Janus House facility in the Bronx. It was a cold weekend in the winter. The members tried contacting Freedom Maintenance to get it fixed, but they couldn't. They called another outfit to do the job. When Jeanette heard about it, he had a conniption fit . . ."

"And after that, the scuttlebutt at Janus House was that Jeanette had some connection with Freedom Maintenance." Escalero interrupted. "It may surprise you, Virgil, but we've already managed to find that out for ourselves."

"Congratulations," I said.

"Thanks. So what you're saying is that Lambert knew about it too."

"Uh-huh."

"How did he find out?"

"From Florence Jackson. She's a switchboard operator at the main Janus House residence."

"What's his connection to her?"

"They got together a few times."

"O.K. So this Florence Jackson told him that there might be a connection between Jeanette and Freedom Maintenance. So what?"

"I'm not sure. I talked to Lambert today. He played dumb about Freedom Maintenance. Why?"

"You tell me," said Escalero.

"He knew enough to recognize the name Freedom Maintenance. He might have known that Jeanette set it up. He might have known about M&M Butchers, and Atlas Laundry too. I don't know. That's what I was trying to find out. Now he's dead."

"You don't even know that, Virgil."

"A body was taken out of his apartment. I think it was Garth Lambert. Who do you think it was?"

"I don't know. I'll find out. Let's say it was Garth Lambert. So what? That and a token will buy you a subway ride."

"Rick, doesn't it strike you as odd that someone who had information pertinent to a murder investigation you're conducting is dead? Don't you want to find out why he died?"

"Virgil, you know the rules. The M.E. already has the body. The law requires an autopsy. You've done your duty as a citizen. You've told me what you know. O.K., I'll get a copy of the autopsy report."

"Look, Rick, if this follows the normal routine, the autopsy might not be done until the day after tomorrow, or later. You might not get a report until Sunday or Monday."

"Virgil," sighed Escalero wearily, "if there's one thing I've learned after eighteen years on the force, it's to keep things simple. I had one suspect in this case. Jeanette. And he committed suicide. I like it that way. You're trying to ring in an accidental death. It just complicates things. I don't see how it helps. Besides, if I hock the M.E. he's liable to call this thing a CUPPI. You can imagine how the Manhattan Homicide cops would like that."

Homicide cops hated CUPPIs. It stood for "Cause Unknown Pending Police Investigation." It meant that the M.E. didn't know why someone died. The cops suspected that the M.E. used it too often, making them get involved in too many unnecessary investigations. Escalero was really fudging. Normal police routine is to concentrate on eliminating all possible suspects until only one was left. Here, they were concentrating on proving Jeanette guilty. It looked like at least some of his powerful contacts were after Jeanette's scalp. Or were throwing him to the wolves. Why not? Jeanette was dead. Life goes on. They were being careful about it. Otherwise, the story about his relatives' partnerships would have broken. But there was no point in talking to Rick about it. I knew he knew it, and he knew I knew it. Besides, there was nothing either of us could do about it.

"How are you doing with Jeanette? How about the opportunity angle? Could he have killed Turley?"

"Oh, he had activities to cover his times, and witnesses to back him up, but they're the kind of witnesses whose stories crack. Don't worry, one or more of them will start singing. If not, we'll turn up physical evidence to put him at the scene of the crime."

"Suppose Jeanette was innocent?" I asked.

Escalero's eyes avoided mine. He said nothing.

"Rick? Suppose he was innocent?"

"That's not our theory," said Escalero.

Jeanette had made lots of enemies in his rise to the

top. He had forced a lot of alliances with people who would just as soon not deal with him. Now he was dead. If enough guys saw this as an opportunity to sever connections with him, and a chance to move in on some of his territory, it would be easy enough for them to pass the word down the grapevine. Nothing crude or drastic. No suppression of evidence. No creation of evidence. No subornation of witnesses. It was a matter of allocation of resources. Put all your manpower on examining Jeanette under a microscope. Try to shake his story. Dig up whatever you can on him. There was no doubt about it: if Jeanette had been innocent, it didn't matter to anyone but me. Then again, he had been the most likely suspect. Which meant he probably hadn't been innocent. "The word's out, right Rick?"

"What word?"

"Get Jeanette."

"Virgil, I don't 'get' anyone. He's the only suspect we have. We're concentrating our efforts on him. That's just good investigatory procedure."

Like hell it was. "You're not calling the shots, are you Rick?"

"Virgil, you know damn well that on a case like this a lieutenant doesn't call the shots."

I remembered Stonebreaker with his skinny frame, bony face, and flat jaw. "It's D.C. Stonebreaker, right?"

"That's who I talk to. I don't know who he talks to. He sets the policy parameters."

"Policy parameters! That's John Jay talk. You mean you won't ask the M.E. to do a rush on this autopsy?"

"You're got to give me a better reason than you have so far."

"Lambert did discuss Freedom Maintenance with Turley."

171

"So what?"

"Turley told him to mind his own business. To finish his work."

"Sure, he didn't want Lambert horning in on his blackmail scheme."

"Or he didn't think there was anything there to begin with. He was following the principles of commercial independent auditors. Have you talked to Wally Post of Post-McBride about that?"

"No."

"You should. Auditors have a somewhat indefinite attitude toward their responsibility for detecting fraud. An ordinary audit done so that an opinion about a financial statement can be given is not designed to uncover fraud."

"So?"

"So Turley was just doing his job. He dismissed the stuff about Freedom Maintenance as gossip. He knew nothing about M&M Butchers or Atlas Laundry. Therefore, he was not blackmailing Jeanette. Therefore, Jeanette did not murder him."

"Then who did, Virgil? Who else had a motive?"

"I don't know. Maybe Lambert did. He didn't like Turley. Turley fired him."

"Or maybe Lambert was killed by Jeanette because he could prove that Jeanette killed . . ." Escalero stopped. "Damn it, Virgil, now you've got me doing it. The odds are overwhelming that Lambert's death was accidental."

"You have to be sure, don't you Rick?"

"Yeah."

"If he was murdered you should know as soon as possible, shouldn't you?"

"Yeah."

"Well?"

"O.K. Virgil, I'm convinced. I'll call the M.E."

"Thanks."

"Don't mention it. Now all I have to do is figure out what I'm going to tell Stonebreaker."

"That shouldn't be a problem, should it?"

"You don't know Stonebreaker. He specifically warned me not to pursue any angles other than Jeanette unless I cleared it with him first."

"So clear it with him."

"I will. After I call the M.E. He'll really chew my ass."

Escalero was O.K.

Chapter 23

It was 8:56 p.m. before Escalero was through with me. I caught a cab back to my Riverside Drive apartment.

A mountain loomed out of the shadows near the entrance. The mountain was Stackhouse, Jeanette's muscle. "You jus' keep walkin' in front of me like everythin's cool, Fletcha'." His right hand was in the pocket of his jacket. The pocket bulged. It could have been a gun. I wasn't going to ask.

It was a gun. A .38. He showed it to me in my apartment. "Yo'll goan be smoked, Fletcha'," he said, "'less yo'll come up with the right answers to ma questions. What happen' to Robie?"

I told him what happened. In greater detail this time. Or at least what I knew. "The cops say it was suicide," I ended.

"She-e-e-e-e-e-t."

"You don't believe it?"

"No way. Ol' Robie no more kill hisself than cat take a bath. I ain't buyin', Fletcha'. You was there alone wi' him. Yo'll onliest one coulda done it. You

174

and me is goan take a little trip. Le's go." He motioned me to the door with his piece.

That was one trip I didn't want to take. But Stackhouse didn't want to hear what I wanted. When we got to the door, I unlocked it, grabbed the outside knob, and flung the door open as fast as I could, wheeling my body to the right around to the front of the door.

"What the h——," Stackhouse got out before I slammed the door in his face and bolted to my right—Stackhouse's left.

"The door flew open again and Stackhouse boiled out, tripping over my extended foot. He sprawled onto the floor of the hall, the gun flying from his hand. I was on his back quick as a cat. That was a mistake. I should have gone for the gun.

Three hard karate chops to his neck had as much effect as trying to put a dent in a steel wall with a wooden mallet. He didn't even bother to shake off the blows. He just stood up, reached over his head, got my whole head in one hand, what felt like my whole shirtfront in the other, and flung me further down the hall, away from the gun. I gave him as much trouble as a cat. A tabby cat.

He came for me, fast. That was a mistake. He should have gone for the gun. I submarined him and kept going down the hall for the gun. I dove for it, rolled over, and sat facing him.

He was already up, but a good ten feet away. I held the gun on him. "I think it'll be easier for me to talk now," I said.

He stood stock still for a moment, as if debating whether to go for me.

"A slug in the kneecap's no mosquito bite," I said.

He shrugged. "Yo'll got the high card, brotha'. What's yo' play?"

175

I motioned him back into the apartment with the gun, and once inside had him sit in an armchair a safe distance from me, both hands plainly in sight on the arms of the chair.

"Did you call Jeanette twice tonight?" I asked.

"Uh-uh."

"Why did he want to speak to you?"

"Business."

It wasn't likely that Stackhouse would tell me what kind of business. It probably didn't matter. But who had called Jeanette before Stackhouse had talked to me on the telephone of the Gamintown Janus House?

"You know the cops are looking for you, right?"

"Uh-huh."

Of course he knew. But I had done my duty as a citizen. Just barely. I needed time to think and I couldn't do it with this gorilla around. All kinds of ideas were knotted in my skull. I needed time to unravel them. I wasn't going to hold him for the cops, it would take too much time. "If I let you go now, do you promise to turn yourself in?"

"Sho' nuff."

Sure he would. When Parrish Enterprises stopped declaring dividends. With Jeanette dead, there'd be a fight to take over his empire. Or divvy it up. In either case Stackhouse didn't want to waste a couple of hours at a station house. Maybe a few hours he was willing to spare, but with a guy like Stonebreaker you never knew. The few hours could become a few days. Stackhouse didn't want to risk that.

I let him go. There's no law that says you have to make a citizen's arrest. Before he left he asked for his gun back. I didn't give it to him. I'd been lucky in our tussle. You never go up against a guy like Stackhouse without some kind of weapon. Unless you have to.

I didn't have to.

Chapter 24

I CALLED my answering service. The message from Janie Fulton, my social worker friend from UASW, said that Marianne Sprague had signed up for two seminars on the afternoon that Turley was killed. One on child abuse. One on abandoned children. The seminars began at 1 p.m. and were over at five.

Scratch one suspect. And my list wasn't too long.

The only other message was from Wally Post of Post-McBride. He wanted me to call him. He left a Suffolk County number. I dialed it.

"Hello?" It was Post.

"Fletcher," I said. "You wanted to talk?"

"Yes, Mr. Fletcher. I received a most unusual call this afternoon. From Garth Lambert. He threatened to blackmail me because he said that I knew about Jeanette's fraudulent activities at Janus House all along. That both myself and Marianne knew."

"Did you?"

"I certainly did not. And if I didn't you know Marianne didn't."

"Why?"

"Oh, come now, Mr. Fletcher, Marianne's a sophisticated, intelligent woman, but she knows nothing about auditing."

"What basis does he have for making the charge?"

"He says that he discussed it with David Turley and Marianne, and that he knows Turley discussed it with Marianne and me."

"Did he say how he knows that?"

"No."

"Did he mention all three outfits or just Freedom Maintenance?"

"All three."

Lambert had only told me his suspicions about Freedom Maintenance. He hadn't mentioned Sprague. "Has he contacted Marianne Sprague?"

"When he called me he said he hadn't. I asked him not to. I don't want her upset with this nonsense. He agreed not to."

"How much did he want?" I asked.

"$50,000."

Lambert was smart in asking Post for it rather than Sprague. If what Lambert believed was true, he stood a much better chance of prying a large sum from Post, who was rich, than from Sprague who, as far as I knew, wasn't. Even if she was rich, she couldn't be as rich as Post.

"Mr. Fletcher, are you still there?"

"Yes."

"I'd like to hire you to handle this matter for us."

"That won't be necessary," I said. I told him why.

"Oh," he said in a hollow and shrunken voice. He hung up.

I took off my jacket, tie, and shoes and stretched out on my bed, mulling over the case. The sticking point was Jeanette's suicide. Did Jeanette really kill himself? I needed an answer. I pictured him as I had last seen him, bigger than life, shaking the salt on the back of his hand, licking it off, downing his tequila, biting into the lime, and smacking his lips with relish. That picture told me something that gave me an answer. An answer from a dead man. I had to be sure that what the picture told me was so. I would have given twenty to one that it was. If it was, Jeanette didn't kill himself.

Billy Jefferson was the strikingly beautiful woman who had been draped over Jeanette when I had met him in his lair at the Manhattan Janus House. She seemed to be the easiest person to tell me what I needed to know. I didn't want to contact Jeanette's family. Too many people would be gathered together sharing their grief. I preferred dealing with one person. Unless I missed my guess, Billy would be alone.

There was only one Billy Jefferson listed in the Manhattan telephone directory. Her address was in Turtle Bay. I dialed her number, told her what I wanted to know, and why. She gave me the answer I expected. It was only two words, but they were the words I wanted to hear. Jeanette wasn't a suicide. Jeanette was murdered. But who did it? I thought I knew, but I couldn't prove it.

I spent the next hour and a half making some more calls.

Chapter 25

I SAVED Escalero for last. He wasn't happy. It was just after midnight and he was on his way home. "Bullshit," he said. "Stackhouse wants us to prove Jeanette was clean. There's no way he can do that. Jeanette killed Turley, and then he killed himself. He knew we were closing in on him. He couldn't stand the idea of jail. He couldn't stand the idea of being on top and then hitting bottom. So he killed himself."

"What about Lambert? What did the autopsy show?"

"He got too much smoke. He was in bed, smoking. He fell asleep and set the mattress on fire. It was an accident, Virgil. It happens all the time."

"Sure. And people get struck by lightning every day. Anything else?"

There was a long pause before Escalero answered. "The autopsy indicated that he had taken a heavy dose of chloral hydrate before he died."

"And that doesn't make you suspicious?"

"There's nothing to indicate that someone else gave it to him. You told me yourself he was having trouble sleeping."

He was. He had told me that. But still, a Mickey Finn? It was next to impossible to detect chloral hydrate when drinking it mixed with any common beverage. On the other hand, it was a relatively common sleeping potion, and easy to get. Anyone who could lay in a supply of grass could just as easily get his hands on chloral hydrate. More easily.

"He hadn't been sleeping," Escalero continued. "He didn't sleep last night. So he took some chloral hydrate to sleep. So what? He was a chain-smoker. There were overflowing ashtrays all over the place. He took the chloral hydrate and went to sleep. He left a butt burning. His mattress caught fire. He was overcome by smoke. Look, Virgil, I even got the Fire Marshall to examine Lambert's apartment."

"That's not the final word," I said.

"You're beating a dead horse, Virgil," he said.

I wasn't. I gave him enough of what I had just put together over the phone to convince him to meet me at Marianne Sprague's apartment.

She lived near me in a brownstone in the eighties off Central Park West. You could say one thing about Marainne Sprague: she wasn't the kind of woman with money who would go to a party and look like all the other women present. Not for her Halston or St. Laurent outfits that were safe and in the height of fashion. She was wearing a diaphanous shocking pink harem costume. Her breasts stood out free from any hindrance behind the sleeveless vest. As a concession to modesty she wore a flesh-colored bikini bottom under the harem pants. I could not tell where her long firm legs ended, and the bikini began. A fluid orange chiffon cape secured by a clasp at her right shoulder flowed around her body to the floor.

"Well, gentlemen, this is a distinct honor and privilege," she said as she opened the door. "Come in. Come in."

She turned back to the interior of the house, and beckoned us to follow. Her cape billowed out behind her as she walked, as silent as a manta ray. I let Escalero go first. I closed the door and brought up the rear. The air-conditioned coolness of the house was a pleasant contrast to the clammy heat of the street.

The living room was as distinctive as her costume. The floors were painted hot orange. The walls were a happy sunshine yellow. A wavy supergraphic imitating an area rug had been painted in lilac, Chinese red, and lime under the clear acrylic coffee table. Moldings and tropic-louver window shutters and closet doors were painted a pure dazzling white. An apartment-sized Stratford sofa covered in a happy cotton-and-linen-blend floral of poppy red, violet, daffodil yellow, and rich forest green on a white ground stood in back of the coffee table. A pair of chrome-framed armless Stratford chairs were placed on either side of the coffee table facing the sofa.

A glass bong with an ivory stem stood on the coffee table. Sprague's bloodshot eyes and spaced-out air told me that she had given it a couple of bangs. I was glad to see it. It meant that things would probably be easier than they might otherwise be. "Now Lieutenant," she said, pointing to the bong, "I hope you won't hold that against me."

We maintained our silence.

She sprawled on the sofa, elbows propped on its back, "Really, boys," she said in a coquettish voice, "I don't see why you come if you're not going to talk."

We sat in the chairs facing her.

Escalero gave her the Miranda.

Her laughter surged up and down octaves in great leaps and squawls. She hooted and snorted and coughed until her eyes filled with tears. Her chest heaved and she bent over double. She stood on her feet and slowly straightened up. She gasped and attempted to take deep breaths, but burst into laughter once more. She strode back and forth with her hands pressed under her rib cage, her face struggling to compose itself. It was no use. Ringing peals of laughter once more poured from her mouth, echoing off the walls. She covered her face with her hands and crossed the room back into the hall.

Escalero followed her.

She came back immediately, laughing harder than ever. It kept on like that for a good five minutes. Great waves of laughter rising and falling, brief moments of respite, further waves, louder and louder, bordering on hysteria. The attack subsided slowly, ending in hiccups and snuffles.

"Oh, god! It hurts my chest," she shouted after she regained her composure. "Excuse me, gentlemen, I just can't help it. What comes next, the spotlight and rubber hoses? I won't need an attorney. I'm a lawyer myself. I think I can handle whatever it is you two gentlemen think you have." Her arrogance combined with the marijuana she had smoked made it impossible for her to admit the need for legal counsel.

Escalero looked at her with astonished eyes. His mind was blown. "Get on with it, Virgil," he said.

She had taken a few bangs on her bong, all right. More than a few. "The game's over, Marianne," I said. "We know you killed Turley. We know you killed Jeanette. We know you killed Lambert."

"Virgil, you sound like you're the one who's been smoking dope," she said. She spoke more slowly than she usually did, slurring her words. "You mean you *think* I did those things, don't you?"

"I know."

"Re-e-e-e-ly?" She put as much sarcasm into it as she could muster.

"When Lambert called you this afternoon, what did he have to say?" She didn't have to answer. I already knew. When I invited Florence to dinner she said that Lambert had sounded as bad as ever, or something like that. It had slipped by me then, but when I was trying to dope things out later at my apartment it hit me: how did she know?

"What makes you think I spoke to him today?"

"Marianne, the call went through the switchboard. You should have thought of that. You should have known Florence would listen. You knew she had a jones for Lambert." Lambert had broken his promise to Post and contacted Sprague. If he hadn't done that he would still be alive. He had probably decided from the way Post reacted that he *hadn't* known what was going on, and if he was going to get money he'd have to tap Sprague directly. He didn't worry about Post blowing the whistle on him because if he did, he'd be blowing it on her too. He was right. Post didn't call the cops. He called me. Florence didn't tell me about the blackmail threat when I first talked to her because she didn't want to get Lambert angry, or in trouble. If he was successful she wanted to share his reward.

"That bothers me, Virgil. It bothers me a lot. Perhaps our most sacred rule at Janus House is to respect each other's privacy. It's very disappointing to learn that a member would eavesdrop. She will be punished for that."

"Not by you she won't. Your punishing days are over."

"You don't really believe that Lambert's pathetic attempt at extortion proves anything, do you?"

"It proves that you were interested enough in M&M

184

Butchers, Atlas Laundry, and Freedom Maintenance to talk to Lambert about them." In our telephone conversation Florence said that when Lambert was doing the audit Sprague had specifically asked him if he noticed anything unusual about the billings from these organizations. After I told Lambert what was unusual about them and how they were connected to Jeanette, he decided to use what he knew to put the squeeze on Sprague and Post. Post hadn't known about Jeanette's scam before I told him, so he sought me out to clear things up. Sprague had killed two people. She decided Lambert was too big a threat to remain alive. If she paid him, he would be standing on her doorstep with his hand held out for the rest of his life. If she didn't pay him, he would talk. The talk would lead the cops down trails they had not explored. Trails that would lead to Marianne Sprague.

"You said you never heard of them, except for that trouble last winter when Freedom Maintenance couldn't be contacted to fix the boiler in the Bronx Janus House," I went on. "You checked out Freedom Maintenance. Found out who owned it. You checked out all the vendors that did business with Janus House. Found out who the owners were, and tied in Atlas and M&M with Jeanette also."

"That's absurd!" she croaked.

"When you asked Lambert about the billings he said he found nothing. He was an accountant. The numbers added up; so as far as he was concerned everything was O.K. He didn't look for what you and I did. Different signatures. Different billing patterns. Different banks of deposit. But once Turley and Jeanette turned up dead, it didn't take a genius to figure you or Post was responsible. Not after I told him about Jeanette's scam."

"I'm surprised at you, Virgil," said Sprague. "Such a

185

fairy tale! Florence is lying. Besides, you say that I killed poor David. And Jeanette. Jeanette was a suicide."

"No he wasn't," I said.

"How can you say that?" she asked.

"Robie Jeanette was left-handed." I figured a south-paw would drink tequila the way Jeanette did, using his left hand, the control hand, to sprinkle the salt on the back of his right hand. Anyway, when I had drunk tequila that time back in Tijuana, I had used my right hand to sprinkle salt on the back of my left. I'm right-handed. My call to Billy Jefferson had proven me right. "You forgot that," I said. "He would never have held the gun in his right hand."

"That's absurd." There wasn't too much conviction in her voice. "If the police thought it was suicide there must have been powder burns. How could I have gotten close enough to hold a gun to his head?"

"Easy. You already knew that Jeanette had left a message at the Manhattan Janus House for Stack-house to call him. You saw it on the switchboard bulletin board when you came in. You checked out the floor plan of the Gamintown Janus House to find out where Jeanette would take the call. You sent Mrs. Dowd on an errand or gave her the day off. You told the switchboard to hold all calls. Florence will verify that. You went out the back way, and drove to the Gamintown Janus House. You used the duplicate set of keys to go in the back way, and hid in that room at the top of the stairs. You waited until you heard a train coming and dialed the number Jeanette had left for Stackhouse. Jeanette sat right in front of the door leading to the room you were hiding in, facing away. Those trains make so much noise you can't hear yourself think, let alone hear a door open. You just stood behind him, held the gun close to his temple, and fired."

"That's ridiculous!" she said.

"When you saw the cop in front of the building you knew you had to kill Jeanette when a train went by. You probably were going to do that anyway so that it would look like suicide. I thought it was strange that the lights on a newly installed telephone bridge didn't work. They didn't work because you unscrewed the light bulb. You did that so Jeanette wouldn't notice that you were using the other extension on the phone he was answering."

"Lieutenant Escalero," she said, "I know of no law that says I have to allow two grown men into my house in the middle of the night just so I can listen to such nonsense."

Escalero stared at her. Hard. But he said nothing.

"You're overlooking one thing," she said. "Mr. Jeanette was all but indicted for David's murder. He was going to jail. Why should I kill him?"

"You killed Turley because he was dropping you and to frame Jeanette for his murder. You figured that way you'd get rid of Jeanette once and for all. Like most murderers, you overlooked all the ramifications of your act. You overlooked the possibility that framing Jeanette might also be the end of Janus House. That your amorous interludes with the Janus House accountants and God knows what else might be broadcast to the world. You had to get Jeanette out of the way as fast as possible to get the story out of the papers as quickly as possible. Even if you couldn't make his death look like a suicide, you figured the cops would look for his murderer among his Gamintown associates. You figured the Janus House part of it would quietly die."

"I don't think I have to dignify such a tale by responding to it," she said. "But you say that I killed poor David Turley, and that creature Lambert also. How could I have? I was attending a lecture when David was killed. In lower Manhattan. Do you think that on my break I found out where David was somehow, inveigled him into a trip to Brooklyn, killed him, got back to Manhattan, all in fifteen minutes?"

"Correction," I said. "You signed up for a seminar. That doesn't mean you attended it." Janie's message had said that Sprague had "signed up" for two lectures on the afternoon of the day Turley was killed. The expression "signed up" had stuck in my head. When I called her back, Janie told me that the practice was for people attending the conference to sign up in advance for the lectures they wished to attend. This was for administrative purposes. To see if the rooms assigned for the various seminars were large enough, to give the chairman advance notice of the affiliations of the people attending the seminar, etc. No attendance was taken, and the fact that someone signed up didn't mean that he had attended.

"What does it mean?" she asked.

"It means that you planned to kill Turley. You couldn't stand his dropping you. It had never happened to you before. If it was just that you probably would have forgotten it. But when you started thinking of killing Turley, you got the idea of blaming Jeanette. You already knew about M&M and those other outfits. You laid a false trail of clues to make it look like Jeanette killed Turley. You typed up that list and taped it to the drawer in his bedroom. That list always bothered me. Who else could have put it there besides you?"

"I admit I've been to David's place," she said, "but what does my love life have to do with . . ."

"You took Jeanette's duplicate set of keys. You

188

knew they'd never be missed. Jeanette wasn't due back to the mother house until the weekend was over. And then you got Turley out to Gamintown on some pretext—'One last favor, David. I want you to see personally what this awful man is doing to me. Look at this terrible place he bought. Listen to those trains. How can we provide therapy here? What can I do?' With Turley dead on the floor of the Gamintown Janus House, and that list in Turley's apartment, you weren't worried about your own alibi too much. After all, who would suspect you? That was a mistake. You're the kind of a person people don't forget. When Lieutenant Escalero questions those other people who signed up for the same seminars as you, he's going to find out that you didn't attend."

Rick nodded.

"And then there's Lambert," I said. "You wanted him out of the way fast. You didn't want him broadcasting the fact that you had suspicions about M&M, Freedom, and Atlas for quite some time. You used the same trick you used to off Jeanette. You had your calls held, slipped out of Janus House the back way, and went to Lambert's apartment. He always felt left out because he wasn't one of the Post-McBride boys you seduced. So you offered yourself to him. You fed him a drink loaded with chloral hydrate, and set fire to his mattress after he passed out. Unfortunately for you, you forgot about Mrs. O'Leary."

"Who?" she asked.

"Lambert's neighbor, Mrs. O'Leary. I escorted her to the lobby away from the smoke from the fire in Lambert's apartment. She complained that because her building had no doorman anyone could walk in. She said she saw two strangers there today. The second one was me. The first one was you. She was throwing her garbage down the incinerator when you stepped off the elevator on Lambert's floor. It was you: red-headed woman clanking with jewelry and wearing a black body stocking, a yellow chiffon skirt, and a vest. That's what you were wearing when I saw you. Why didn't you hold that group therapy session?"

She shrugged. "Something came up. I had to cancel it."

"You canceled it so you could snuff Lambert."

She stared straight ahead, saying nothing.

Rick stood up and said, "I'm going to book you, Miss Sprague."

Chapter 26

SHE hired the city's best criminal lawyer. The same one Jeanette had hired, Earl Cosgrove. He couldn't help her much. Not after the cops started working up her case.

In February 1976, one Muriel Spencer had made requests for the partnership papers of eleven vendors doing business with Janus House from the County Clerks in New York, the Bronx, Queens, and Brooklyn. These were all the organizations set up as partnerships that did business with Janus House. A signature verification expert said that all of the Muriel Spencer signatures were in Marianne Sprague's handwriting.

Two people had seen her leave the premises of Hudson College at 1 p.m. on the afternoon Turley was killed. Two others saw her return at about four. Her car, a canary yellow Porsche, was seen the same day in the back driveway of the Gamintown Janus House by a family of welfare squatters who lived in one of the abandoned buildings behind the Gamintown Janus House.

The cop stationed in front of the house had seen

the same car circling the block at about 9:45 on the morning Jeanette was killed. At 9 a.m. on the same morning she sent Mrs. Dowd on an errand to pick up some research material at Columbia University. She told her to take the rest of the day off when this chore was completed. Florence testified that all her calls were held at the switchboard from 9:10 to 11:15 a.m. and from 2:10 to 3:30 p.m. Florence further stated that she had listened from the switchboard to Lambert's blackmail demand to Sprague.

Her fingerprints were found on the back door of the Gamintown Janus House and on the receiver of the telephone she used to call Jeanette to his death. The light bulb in the phone had been unscrewed.

The same gun killed both Jeanette and Turley.

Mrs. O'Leary identified her as the woman she had seen in the hallway of her building on the day Lambert was killed.

She was sentenced to three concurrent life terms.

The Janus House program was discontinued; the members transferred to various other drug rehabilitation programs throughout the City.

I drove Chantal Montez to Kennedy the day she left to return to the coast. The ordeal of losing both her brother and her lover in less than a month did not rob her of her quiet strength. Or her dignity. Or her beauty.

When it was time for her to board, she said, "Adiós Virgil. *Gracias*. We will see each other again."

I hoped she was right. If I had anything to do with it, she would be.

I went up to the observation deck and watched her plane, until, a tiny speck, it disappeared over the horizon.